BIKER'S GIRL 2
ON THE RUN

by

LIA ANDERSSEN

Published by **CHIMERA**
ISBN 9781780804712

This work is sold subject to the condition that it shall not, by way of trade or otherwise, be lent, resold, hired out or otherwise circulated without the publisher's prior written consent in any form of binding or cover other than that in which it is published, and without a similar condition being imposed on the subsequent purchaser. The author asserts that all characters depicted in this work of fiction are eighteen years of age or older, and that all characters and situations are entirely imaginary and bear no relation to any real person or actual happening.

Copyright Lia Anderssen. The right of Lia Anderssen to be identified as author of this book has been asserted in accordance with section 77 and 78 of the Copyrights Designs and Patents Act 1988.

This novel is fiction - in real life practice safe sex.

Chapter One

The day was already warm, the early morning sunlight penetrating the canopy of trees and shedding a dappled light on the grass below. The wood made a perfect setting of peaceful bliss. The only sound was that of the river as it swept gently by, small wavelets lapping at the river banks. A group of rabbits sat by its edge, nibbling at the grass, and in the sky above the occasional bird call was audible. The scene was idyllic, and apparently untouched by humans.

But this rural spot, despite initial appearances, was not deserted.

Indeed there was unmistakable evidence of the presence of man. In a small clearing close to the river's edge something gleamed brightly in the sun, looking strangely out of place in this green and pleasant setting. It was a motorcycle. A large, powerful machine with thick, rounded tyres and wide upswept exhausts, a leather jacket draped carelessly from the handlebars. Its presence among the flowers and trees was enough to make any casual observer stop and stare, and to wonder what it was doing there.

The bike was, however, not the only thing that gave a somewhat incongruous air to the scene. Beside it lay a figure in the grass. A figure that would have captivated anyone who encountered it.

It was a girl, slim and beautiful, with an air of youthful innocence about her that made her seem very vulnerable as she blinked her eyes, clearly waking from a deep sleep. She was totally naked, her firm breasts tipped with large brown nipples that pointed up to the treetops. Her waist was slim, her belly flat, her legs long and slender. But there was something else about her. Something that would have turned the head of any red-blooded male who stumbled across her. Her pubic mound was completely shaved, so that lying as she was, with her legs spread slightly apart, the full pink lips of her sex were totally exposed.

The girl stretched languorously in the soft grass, then sat up and gazed about.

"Thorkil?"

As she called the name there was a rustling in the grass nearby and a young man emerged. He was tall, well over six foot, his hair hanging in golden tresses that reached to his shoulders. He was clad in a leather biking suit, the zipper open almost to the waist. He crossed to where she sat, and stood gazing down at her.

"Did you sleep well?"

"Mmm. I just went straight out."

"After the way you were behaving last night I should think you were tired out."

She blushed. "You did enjoy me, didn't you?"

"Very much," he smiled. "Now come on, we really should be getting back on the road."

"Where are we going?"

"Back to my base."

"Your base?"

"Yes. Depot twenty-nine."

"Depot twenty-nine? What's that?"

"That's where I live. And that's where we'll be going after I've checked in with some friends."

"What friends?"

"Very good friends. I'm sure you'll like them."

"And that's where we're going now?"

"Yes."

The girl rose to her feet, glancing nervously about. It was as if she had only now become aware of her nudity, and was suddenly feeling very exposed. "Isn't there something I could wear?" she asked.

He shook his head. "Not unless you know how to weave leaves together."

She lowered her eyes. "You mean I'm to stay naked?"

He grinned. "I prefer you like that."

"But surely if I'm to meet your friends..."

He moved close to her, running his hand gently over her breast. "I expect they will like you naked too."

"But Thorkil..."

He placed a hand over her mouth. "There's nothing more to say," he murmured.

For a second she looked as if she might protest. Then she sighed and shrugged her shoulders. If that was the way he wanted it, then it was not for her to object. The decision was a sensible one. After all, it was to him that she owed her freedom. He it was who had tried his best to buy her imprest, but had been cheated out of it. And more to the point, it was he who had rescued her from the Black Cat, and from the clutches of the dreadful Helda, who had sold her body to anyone able to pay for it. All this meant that she belonged to Thorkil now, and would do whatever he wished.

The girl's name was Lia. She had been captured by the Bikers more than four months earlier, while on the run after nearly killing the warden of the hostel where she had lived. A group of Bikers found her wandering along the highway naked, trying to buy a ride in a truck with her body. The Bikers claimed her, selling her imprest at auction to Helda, the cruel owner of the Black Cat. There she had been kept as a plaything for men and women alike, permanently naked. Shaved and available to be chained, beaten or taken by anyone who could afford the price.

Then, just the night before, she had been rescued by her knight in shining armour, Thorkil.

Thorkil, like Helda, was a Biker. The Bikers had ruled the highways since law and order all but broken down years before, leaving the cities as nightmarish areas where crime was rife and to venture out at night without protection had become extremely dangerous. The Bikers' great service depots were scattered all over the country, each a tribal area in its own right. In these places young men and women were pressed into service to repair and maintain the great trucks that roved the highways. Outside the cities the Bikers were in charge, the genuine law enforcement officers simply paying lip service to their jobs, content with the backhanders they received from the men and women in black leather.

And now, in Thorkil's hands, Lia was a Biker's girl.

Thorkil reached out for her hand, pulling her to him. She stepped forward willingly, turning her face up to his as he closed his lips over hers. She felt his tongue force its way between her lips and opened her mouth to accept it, licking it with her own tongue as she pressed her naked body against him, rubbing her crotch against his strong thigh.

They kissed for a full minute, then he broke away. "Suck me," he ordered, his voice full of quiet authority.

Lia was used to obeying, and she did not hesitate. At once she dropped to her knees before him, looking for all the world like one kneeling in front of an idol in worship. She reached eagerly for his zip, and tugged it down until the suit fell open.

Underneath he was naked, his body muscular and tanned. She gazed at him for a moment in admiration, taking in the broad chest, with its scattering of golden curls, and his lean torso.

His cock was long and fat and hung down from his groin, still dormant. Lia took it in her fingers. It felt warm and soft, and she squeezed it gently, cupping his heavy balls with her other hand.

Raising her head, she took him into her mouth and began to suck him. His manhood tasted salty, and the smell of him sent a thrill through her as she contemplated what was about to happen.

Almost at once she felt his penis begin to swell, filling her open mouth. She stroked his balls, happy to be kneeling subserviently before her Biker and doing his will. He took hold of her head and pressed it to his groin, and she responded at once, sucking harder, taking it further inside, flicking her tongue back and forth over the tip as it stiffened to its full size.

Once he was hard she began in earnest, bobbing her head up and down as she sucked hungrily, his cock sliding in and out of her mouth, her saliva dribbling down its thick shaft. In response he gave a low moan and pressed her harder against him. Lia glanced up at him momentarily. His eyes were closed and his head was thrown back, his expression intent. The sight of his obvious arousal spurred her on, and she felt a wetness begin to seep through her sex as she pleasured him.

Suddenly he withdrew from her mouth, his weapon wet and glistening. She looked up questioningly.

"Over the bike seat. Face down."

4

Lia sprang eagerly to her feet and scurried across to where Thorkil's bike stood. She approached it from behind, lowering her body forward over it. The plastic seat felt warm in the sunshine and her nipples tingled as they brushed against its surface. She flattened herself onto it, her lovely rounded backside thrust backwards and upwards, ready for penetration. For a fleeting moment she felt a pang of shame, and wondered what he must think of her lasciviousness. There had been no hesitation whatsoever in her actions, and there was no doubting her desire. She wanted desperately to feel him inside her, and would obey his every whim.

But there was no time now for prudishness. With a gasp she felt his hands slide up her inner thighs towards the very centre of her pleasure.

His fingers prised apart the cheeks of her bottom, laying her open for his inspection. She groaned as she felt his fingers trace the crevice of her behind, stroking the tight star of her anus before working lower to the hot pink slit that gaped so invitingly.

He slid two fingers inside her, making her body start as the pleasure overwhelmed her. He began to frig her, his fingers making a slight squelching sound as they moved in and out of her. Lia remained where she was, her cheek pressed against the bike seat, biting her lower lip to prevent herself from crying aloud with pure lust. At last she could bear it no more. "Fuck me Thorkil," she cried.

He smiled. "Ask me nicely."

"P-please fuck me Thorkil."

"Again."

"Oh! Oh please fuck me. Please put your cock into me, Thorkil. Fuck me!"

The last word was almost lost in a strangled cry as she felt the bulb of his glans pressing against her slit. She pushed her backside at him eagerly, and with a cry felt him slide his cock into her, deeper and deeper until it filled her completely.

Then he was fucking her. Driving his thick weapon hard into her, his stomach slapping against her backside as he took his pleasure in her. Lia was beside herself with passion. He was giving her precisely what she craved. The night before he had been gentle and loving, but now he was simply taking what was rightly his, ramming his cock into her with an almost animal urgency, and she realised with a shock that that was the way she preferred it. To be utterly his and prey to his every whim.

The force of his thrusts became harder, pounding her body, and she began to fear that the cycle might fall over. She clung to the tank as tight as she was able, her breath coming in loud grunts as she was hurled forward with every stroke.

He gave a shout, and she felt his sperm pumping into her. Almost at once her own orgasm was triggered and she too was crying aloud as her lustful desires overcame her. Sensing her passion he continued to plunge his great cock deeper as it spurted again and again within her. She wanted to laugh and cry at the same time, such was the pleasure of her own climax and her stomach slapped wetly against the plastic of the bike seat as he rode her down the slope from her peak, slowing gently as the pleasure began to gently ebb.

At last he was still and she lay panting beneath him, exhausted. His fingers traced her spine as he gazed down, his cock still embedded within her.

"My passionate little Biker's girl," he murmured.

Chapter 2

At the Black Cat Helda was watching as the third of the three gatekeepers who had allowed Lia to escape slumped to the floor, his teeth and jaw broken, his eyes blackened, his nose a bloody pulp. She kicked him twice in the ribs, each blow resounding to the crack of broken bone. She turned and left the servants to drag the three groaning men back to their cells.

She strode back to her office and slumped into the chair behind her desk. She leaned forward and pressed a bell. Almost immediately her assistant Stefan was with her.

"Is the transmitter working?" she asked anxiously.

"Oh yes. Did you get someone in Thorkil's camp to attach it to his machine?"

"Of course. You didn't think I'd risk him getting away with her, did you?" she snapped. "Oh no, I still have plans for that young lady! So where are they?"

"About twenty-five miles down the highway. They seem to have pulled off into some woods."

"Good. They're bound to join up with the rest of his cronies. Set an ambush for when they arrive there. We'll leave them to their fun for now. After all, there's plenty of time."

A thin, evil smile began to play about her lips.

Lia clung hard to Thorkil as they roared down the road. He rode the machine hard, leaning low into bends, then grabbing a handful of throttle as they straightened up so that she had to hug close to him to avoid being flung off the back. The machine was a large one, and the thrill of the speed accompanied by the vibration of the engine induced an almost sexual pleasure in the naked girl as they sped along. Her arousal was increased by the other drivers on the road, who would point in fascination at her lovely young body as they passed, grinning and making rude gestures at the sight of her. Lia in return would grin back, sometimes thrusting her lovely arse back at them, making their eyes wide with desire.

They rode on for many miles before the bike slowed. Then they were swinging left, off into the wooded countryside with which Lia was becoming familiar since falling into the hands of the Bikers.

They followed a track that wound through the trees for about a mile. The whole area seemed deserted, and Lia wondered where he could possibly be taking her. Then the track widened into a clearing, in the centre of which was a group of black-clad figures.

Thorkil braked to a halt and cut the engine, the sudden silence taking Lia by surprise. It took her ears a second to accustom themselves to the quiet of the wood.

They had come to a halt by a group of bikes parked under a tree. Thorkil kicked down the stand and climbed off. Lia sat where she was, nervous and embarrassed as she looked across at the group in the clearing.

"Who are they?" she asked timidly.

"Just friends. Friends who assisted me in getting you out. They're all looking forward to meeting you."

"But I'm naked."

He looked at her rather sternly. "Listen," he said, "you are a beautiful and sexy girl, and I rescued you because I want you, and I believe you want me. Am I right?"

"You know you are."

"Then you must realise the role of a Biker's girl. It is to serve her man in whatever way he pleases. If I choose that my friends see you naked, then that is what will happen."

She hung her head. "Yes Thorkil," she mumbled.

He wrapped his arms around her and kissed her. "Good," he said.

She looked into his eyes. "Must I always obey you?"

"Yes. Unless and until you gain your leathers. Then you become a Biker yourself. But that will take some time."

"How long?"

He placed a finger on her lips. "Enough questions for now. Come and meet my friends."

She followed him across the clearing, her face glowing with embarrassment as they approached the group. Somehow her position at the Black Cat, as a plaything, had made her enforced nudity easier to bear. Here she was being asked to meet Thorkil's friends in an otherwise fairly normal social situation, and her lack of clothes made her feel very conspicuous indeed.

There were six Bikers, all sitting on logs about a small fire. They looked up and waved to Thorkil as they came closer, and Lia realised with surprise that two of them were girls. They were dressed the same as the men, indicating that they had 'gained their leathers', as Thorkil had described. The presence of the females only served to increase her discomfort. The contrast between their bodies, clad in the black one-piece leather suit that many Bikers wore, and her own, totally exposed, her breasts and sex bare for all to see, seemed to make her the more conspicuous.

They came to a halt in front of the group. "This is Lia," said Thorkil.

All eyes were on her, and she wanted to turn away. Clearly Thorkil sensed this.

"Stand straight," he ordered. "Legs apart. Hands behind your head." Reluctantly Lia took up the familiar submissive stance before the six pairs of eyes, her legs spread so that her shaven sex was open to their gaze.

One of the men whistled. "Very nice, Thorkil," he said. "I can see why you wanted to rescue her."

Thorkil sat down on the log. "Yeah. Quite something isn't she?"

"Stunning," said one of the girls.

"Really sexy," said the other.

Thorkil waited until they'd all had a look, then sensing Lia's embarrassment changed the subject.

"Now what about something to eat?" he said.

As he spoke Lia realised she was extremely hungry. Resting in the embers of the fire was a cooking pot, and there was a wonderful smell coming from it. One of the men lifted the lid to reveal a steaming stew. He grabbed a ladle and scooped two large portions into bowls. He passed one across to Thorkil, then offered the other to Lia. She glanced down quizzically to Thorkil, who gave a little nod. Unclasping her hands from behind her head she took the bowl and, still standing, began spooning the food into her mouth. The stew was hot and tasty, and she consumed every morsel, drinking the last of the gravy from the bowl before placing it at her feet and putting her hands behind her head once more.

The Bikers began to talk amongst themselves and Lia stood, passively listening to their conversation. Thorkil described in detail how the escape had gone, and the six Bikers attended with interest, firing questions at him all the time. One of the men, though, seemed unable to take his eyes off Lia. He was short and balding slightly, a pink patch of skull showing through at the back of his dark, lank hair. She could tell from his belly that he was a beer drinker, and he confirmed this by frequently swigging from a can that sat on the grass beside him. Lia gathered from the chat that his name was Rico.

Once Thorkil's story had been told they turned to her, and began to question her about her life at the Black Cat. Rico in particular was curious and Lia found herself blushing deeply as she was made to describe the sex and punishments she had experienced. Throughout Thorkil was silent, and she wondered what he must be thinking of her.

At last they seemed to have heard enough, and to Lia's surprise Rico rose to his feet and took her arm.

"You're quite a girl," he said.

She dropped her eyes. "Thank you."

He took her chin in his hand, turning her face to his. "Now what about coming and having a little fun with me?"

She stared at him. How could he ask such a thing? And in front of Thorkil as well!

"What do you mean?" she asked.

"What do you think I mean? Here you are, starkers, that shaven pussy of yours displayed for all to see. It makes me horny as hell. Now come on."

"No!" She pulled away from him. "Thorkil..."

Thorkil looked up at her. "Rico is a good friend," he said. "Without his help I'd never have traced you to the Black Cat. He's earned your gratitude."

"But you can't make me go with him," said Lia in dismay.

"Is that how a Biker's girl talks to her man?"

The words came from one of the two girl Bikers. She was called Lara, tall and slim with magnificent breasts and flowing blonde hair. She rose and joined Rico.

"I reckon you're going soft, Thorkil."

"She's new," he replied. "She'll soon learn her place."

"Even so," replied Lara, "talking back to you like that should at least earn her a smacked arse."

"All right," said Thorkil. "But just six, mind."

Lia stared at him. A smacked bottom? After all she'd been through he was going to have her bottom smacked like some recalcitrant schoolgirl? She opened her mouth to protest, then caught his eye and saw a dark look cross his face. She closed her lips and hung her head. Of course it was her at fault, not Thorkil. He had explained her position only a few minutes before, and already she'd forgotten. She was a Biker's girl now, and as such must respect her position. To defy Thorkil in front of his companions was to undermine his stature in the group, and that was something she knew he could never allow. She relaxed and stood passively awaiting her orders.

Lara took her hands and turned her round, so she was facing away from the fire. Then she pulled her gently forward, bending her over until her palms rested on the log on which they had been sitting. She shoved Lia's legs apart, presenting her rear beautifully to those watching. Once in position Lia kept her body as still as she could, her eyes fixed on the ground,

"You gonna whack her, Thorkil?" asked Lara.

"No, you go ahead," he replied. He sounded nonchalant, and Lia turned her head to look at him. He gave her a slight smile and winked, and she knew he was no longer angry with her.

Smack!

Lara's hand came down flat on the left cheek of Lia's backside. The blow stung, but she held her position.

Smack!

This time her right cheek was assaulted, the blow cracking down onto her tender flesh. But now the pain triggered another feeling. As so often in the past the humiliation and pain of her punishment ignited a perverse spark of arousal, and she felt the muscles of her sex convulse slightly as she anticipated the next blow.

Smack!

The third blow caught the underside of her pretty behind, rocking her body so that her dangling breasts shook tantalisingly. Her bottom was smarting dreadfully and she could imagine how it must look, the hand-mark reddening as the others watched.

Smack!

The fourth blow fell precisely where the first had, doubling the pain in the hapless girl's bottom. She'd been spanked many times since originally falling into the hands of the Bikers, and a spanking from a girl was far from the worst punishment she had received, but Lara was striking with deadly accuracy and the pain was very real. And so was the arousal, the juices within her beginning to flow as her ordeal went on.

Smack!

It was all Lia could do to prevent herself crying out as Lara's hand caught her once more. She closed her eyes as she awaited the last blow.

Smack!

Lara's hand descended for the sixth time onto Lia's backside. Then it was over and the girl was helping her to straighten up. Lia's bum stung terribly, and she knew it must be bright red. But the heat in her bottom was as nothing to that in her belly, and the shortness of her breath was more a panting desire than anything else. Lia was extremely aroused, and she knew that the evidence was visible to all on the glistening lips of her sex as she turned to face them.

"Wow!" Rico grinned. "That's turned her on. Look at her!"

Lia's face glowed almost as red as her behind as she felt her nether lips twitch once more. She turned to Thorkil, who rose to his feet, and taking her in his arms kissed her on the lips. She responded eagerly to his kiss, pressing against him, her entire body alive with lust, but he broke away.

"Rico," he said shortly, and nodded to her.

She gave Thorkil a lingering look, then turned to face Rico. He reached out his hand and she placed hers into it. She felt her other hand grasped and turned to see Lara on her other side.

"I'm coming too," she said. "I want a bit of this action."

Chapter 3

Lia glanced back over her shoulder towards Thorkil as she was led away by Rico and Lara. He gave her a small wave, then turned back and continued talking to the others. Lia's mind was in a whirl. On the one hand she was surprised that he was able to just stand and calmly watch as she was taken away like this. He must know what the two Bikers' intentions were, but he was seemingly unworried. At the same time she was slightly shocked by her own feelings. She knew she should be protesting, fighting to escape from this pair, but all she could feel was the most extraordinary thrill.

They made their way towards the spot where the bikes were parked, and for a moment she thought they were going to drive her away. But they passed the gleaming machines and made instead for the trees.

They entered the wood by a narrow path, barefoot Lia treading gingerly as she was led along. They didn't go far, just to a small clearing about fifty yards from the one they had left. In the centre was a fallen tree trunk about three feet in diameter.

"Sit down on there," ordered Rico, indicating the trunk.

The two released her hands and Lia approached it nervously, turning to face them and lowering her sore backside onto the rough wood. Rico and Lara stood side by side watching her, and she gazed quizzically back at them waiting to discover what they wanted.

"Open your legs," said Rico.

Slowly Lia did as she was told, spreading her legs wide so that her bare sex was once again exposed to the two watchers.

"Play with yourself."

"What?"

"You heard me. Play with yourself. Get those delectable nipples of yours erect first."

"But I..."

"No buts. You've been wandering about flaunting yourself enough. Now let's see some action."

Lia looked from one to the other. She felt extremely embarrassed by Rico's demand, yet at the same time there was a warm sensation spreading within her as she felt their eyes on her body. She hesitated for a moment longer, then slowly moved her hands up to her breasts. She took them, one in each hand, and began gently to caress them. Her fingers rubbed the soft flesh and her nipples began to respond, the brown buds puckering to hardness to stand out invitingly from her firm globes.

Her fingers worked on, caressing and kneading, and in no time at all her own caresses began to have the effect they had wanted on her, and her face was a picture of rapt concentration as she continued her self-arousal.

"Now your cunt."

Once again she looked wide-eyed at Rico.

"Your cunt," he said again.

"Frig yourself, you randy little slut."

Lia didn't need to be told again. While her left hand continued to play with her breasts, her right reached eagerly for her open slit. She slid her fingers down over her pubic mound, giving a little start when they came in contact with her clitoris. She eased it out from between her sex lips, flicking gently as it came erect. When it was hard and visible she raised her eyes to Rico's and let her fingers run lower over the wet surface of her slit. Gently she prised apart her nether lips, exposing the pinkness inside. Once more she paused, her eyes fixed on Rico's, then her hand moved again, her elegant digits delving into her aching love hole.

Lia knew she had her audience spellbound, and it had been her intention to tease the watching pair with her lascivious actions for as long as possible. But once she penetrated herself the familiar lustful feelings returned and she felt her control slip away.

She began to frig herself, her fingers working in and out, making a slight squelching sound as they did so. Her body responded enthusiastically to the sensation and she found herself opening her legs still wider as her passion overcame her. She planted her feet firmly on the ground and raised her bottom off the tree, thrusting her sex forward as her fingers slid in and out. Her breath was coming in short gasps as she masturbated, her whole self concentrated on the delicious sensations her fingers were creating.

"Stop."

For a moment Lia did not obey, being too intent on her own pleasure.

Whack!

Rico had removed his belt and used it to deliver a stinging blow across the naked girl's thighs. It caught Lia by surprise and she stopped masturbating at once, looking up startled at her companions, her face redder than ever. She wondered at the sight she must make, stretched there totally nude, her breasts swollen, the nipples hard as nuts, her legs spread wide so they could watch the convulsions of her sex lips as they tried to close about an imaginary cock.

"Jeez," said Lara. "Thorkil told us you were hot, but you've surpassed yourself. That little slit of yours looks like it would positively eat a cock if it could. And speaking of eating things..."

As she spoke she moved to Lia, pushing her back gently so that she lay across the trunk, her back arched, her breasts forced up. Lia made no protest, allowing the female Biker to manipulate her body into the position she wanted. Then she felt Lara's lips close over her nipples and gave a cry of pleasure.

Lara took hold of Lia's left breast, squeezing it as she sucked noisily on the nipple. Lia squirmed with pleasure, which doubled when she felt Rico's mouth close over the other one.

His hand reached for Lia's shaven pussy, eliciting another cry from his naked captive as he slid his fingers into her warm, wet love hole. Lia pressed her crotch against his hand, her body arched upwards as the two Bikers took possession of her young body. Once again her control was lost as she writhed beneath their hands and mouths, totally abandoned to her own pleasure, her juices flowing down her thighs.

"Wow," gasped Lara as she lifted her mouth from Lia's swollen nipple. "This bitch is something else. I just gotta have her lick me." She rose to her feet, reaching for the zipper at her throat, pulling it all the way down and round her crotch almost to the top of her backside while Lia looked on, her heart thumping with anticipation.

Lara peeled off her suit. Underneath she was naked and Lia felt the hotness within her increase as she surveyed Lara's lovely body. Her breasts were magnificent, the biggest Lia had ever seen, yet barely drooping at all. The nipples were large and prominent and projected slightly upwards. Beneath them her body curved in to a trim waist, then widened again, her hips in perfect proportion to her breasts. Lia fixed her eyes on Lara's crotch. Her pubic mound was a mass of blonde curls below which her sex lips showed thick and prominent. Lara stretched herself in the sun, arching her body proudly, clearly enjoying the attention it was receiving from her two companions. Then she moved closer to Lia again, but this time approaching from above her head, standing so that her legs straddled Lia's face as she stood gazing down at her.

All Lia could see was Lara's pink slit hovering just above her face. Then as she watched Lara began lowering herself onto her mouth.

"Right," she said, "it's your turn. Lick me, you randy little bitch. Get that tongue of yours working."

Lia had little choice, but even if she had been given one the result would have been the same. Lara's sex descended and her senses were filled with the sight and smell of a woman's arousal. Tentatively she protruded her tongue, running it gingerly over the soft lips of Lara's slit. As she did so the Biker gave a groan and pressed herself down harder.

Lia sought out the girl's clitoris, lapping at it and flicking it back and forth with darting movements of her tongue. She felt the little bud swell and took it gently between her teeth, sucking it in between her lips. Lara gave a little cry and Lia felt her hips move back and forth. The supine girl reached her arms up and around Lara's thighs, her hands grasping the woman's buttocks. This allowed her to control her movements better and to coordinate herself with the pumping of Lara's hips.

Lia felt the fingers slide out of her sex, then something else probing her. For a second she abandoned Lara's pussy and gazed down between her breasts. Rico had unzipped his suit to the crotch, and beneath his heavy beer gut she could see his cock jutting proudly erect. She gave a little moan of pleasure, which was stifled as Lara pressed down onto her face once more.

Lia spread her legs as wide apart as she was able, raising her bottom from the wood as she willed Rico to penetrate her. She gave a gasp as she felt him shove his hips forward and he was inside her, his cock filling her as he rammed it home. Rico began working his hips back and forth as he took his pleasure in her. Above her Lara moaned and wriggled as Lia's tongue went to work, probing her vagina, the sleek little muscle worming deep into the Biker's throbbing slit.

Lia's arousal was intense. She reached a hand up to feel for Lara's breast, only to find Rico's already there, squeezing and mauling at his fellow Biker while shafting Lia hard.

Together the three of them made an extremely erotic sight. The lovely young girl stretched backwards across the tree trunk, her hair hanging down, her face buried in the other woman's crotch as she slurped noisily at it. Lara was pumping her hips back and forth, pressing down on her lover's face whilst locked in a passionate embrace with Rico. Their lips were pressed together in a bruising kiss, their tongues intertwined as he stroked her magnificent breasts, and all the time he was thrusting his cock into Lia, fucking her for all he was worth.

Lara's moans were turning to cries, and the juice flowed from her, dribbling down Lia's cheeks as she tried to lap it all up. Rico's cock was pumping harder and harder, and Lia knew she could not hold back much longer.

Rico came first, his cock throbbing as he unleashed his load into Lia's love hole. He gave a groan of pleasure, which was echoed almost at once by Lara, her cunt muscles twitching uncontrollably as her orgasm overcame her. All this was too much for Lia and she too let herself go, the pleasure flowing through her in waves as she screamed her pleasure into Lara's open sex.

For a second it was as if the three of them were frozen. Locked together cock to cunt, mouth to cunt and mouth to mouth, their bodies joined in a crescendo of pleasure that seemed to flow from one to another like some strange electric energy. Then with a collective gasp they let go, Lara and Rico collapsing into each others' arms as Lia flopped, her tired muscles slowly relaxing as she lay back, gasping for breath.

She remained where she was, watching as Rico pulled up his zipper and Lara climbed back into her leathers. She knew she must look a sight, her face glistening with Lara's come whilst Rico's sperm was streaked down her thighs. But she didn't care. She was proud of herself. All that mattered to her now was that she was a Biker's girl, Thorkil's girl. And it was for him alone that she gave herself so freely to whoever it pleased him to offer her to.

Rico and Lara took her hands again, pulling her to her feet. She rubbed her backside, brushing off the scraps of bark and grass that stuck to it. The redness had faded, but it still felt sore to the touch. Nothing was said as they made their way back to the camp. Lia wandered dreamily along between them, anxious to be back with Thorkil, her body glowing with pleasure.

They had almost broken into the clearing when they heard the bikes. The roar of powerful engines was unmistakable and Rico and Lara stopped in their tracks.

"What the hell?" said Rico, startled. "Where are they going?"

"Hang on," said Lara. "Those aren't our bikes."

They began to run, dragging Lia along between them. As they broke cover into the clearing they saw the source of the sound. It was a group of about fifteen Bikers, speeding across the clearing, away from where the three were standing, bearing down on the small group by the fire.

"Oh shit," said Lara. "It's Helda."

Chapter 4

Lia stood frozen to the spot as she watched the Bikers tear across the clearing, their machines roaring deafeningly as they rode helter-skelter towards the group gathered around the fire. All wore the familiar black leathers of Bikers, but the insignia on their backs was different from that sported by Thorkil and his companions. She recognised it instantly as the logo used by Helda, and at that very moment she realised with a start that the figure leading the attack was indeed Helda herself.

"Quick," shouted Rico, "let's get them." He set out at a run in the direction of his companions, but Lara held back momentarily. She could see they were hopelessly outnumbered. It was also clear to her why Helda was attacking. She turned to face Lia.

"Listen," she said, "there's too many of them to fight. It's you they're after, so you've got to get the hell out of here."

"But where?" asked Lia, despairingly.

"It doesn't matter where. Can you ride a bike?"

Lia nodded. They had taught her to ride during her time at the Black Cat. Some of the clients found it a turn-on to be picked up by a naked biker. Helda invented a scenario by which the man was walking along the road, hitching, and Lia would ride up and offer him a lift. Then she would speed around the estate with the man perched behind her, his hands roaming over her body while she drove. The final act would always involve her parking the machine in some remote corner and submitting to his desires. This little piece of playacting had become extremely popular with the Black Cat's customers, and soon Lia was riding with some skill. Now, ironically, it appeared that the biking tuition would prove to be her salvation.

Lara dragged her across to where the bikes were parked. The attacking Bikers were still concentrating on the group round the fire, and had so far failed to notice the two women. She pulled one of the bikes off its stand.

"Get on," she ordered.

Lia swung a leg over the machine and took hold of the handlebars. As she did Lara kicked the starter and the engine roared into life. Then she slapped Lia's bare behind.

"Right, on your way!" she shouted. Lia opened her mouth to ask where, but Lara was already running towards the scrimmage in the centre of the clearing.

Lia engaged first gear and let go of the clutch. Too fast. The machine reared up onto its back wheel and for a moment she feared she would lose it. She closed the throttle, letting the front wheel drop again, then twisted it open and was moving, skidding the bike around and heading for the track along which they had come.

She glanced over her shoulder and her heart sank. One of the Bikers had spotted her and was already heading after her at high speed. Despite her skill at handling the machine she had no doubt that his would be greater.

Lia slowed her bike and glanced back again, anxious to see how close the other rider was. As she did so she noticed Lara, between her and the other Biker, running across to intercept the man. For a second it looked as if Lara would be mown down by the speeding cycle, but at the last minute she sprang aside and thrust something into the man's front wheel. At once the wheel locked up, sending the bike sideways and flinging the rider off into the dust. Lia offered a little prayer of thanks and crouched low over the handlebars of her machine as she sped away down the track.

She had to think fast. She knew that the advantage she had gained was only a temporary one, and that she would easily be outridden by Helda and her men once they realised where she was going. Her only hope was to get off the beaten track and drive deeper into the wood. She checked the road ahead. To her left there was a small clearing and she slowed as she approached it. Sure enough there was a game track, winding off into the depths of the wood. She braked the machine almost to a stop and turned in slowly, anxious that there be no mark in the road to betray where she had left it. Then she was on the path and plunging down through the trees.

Negotiating the track took all the skill she could muster. The trees hung low and there were obstacles around every bend. On more than one occasion she came within a hair's breadth of striking something, or sliding into the undergrowth. But she stayed on, her teeth gritted in grim determination as she penetrated ever deeper into the wood.

The vegetation was no more than a green blur, so fast was Lia travelling. The path twisted this way and that, and she fought hard to stay in control of the machine as she sped along. She had no idea how far she had travelled. Five miles? Ten? All she knew was she was getting away, putting as much distance as she could between herself and Helda.

It was some time before she felt secure enough to slow her pace. She eased back the throttle and looked about. For the first time she wondered where she might be. There were no landmarks she could recognise. Perhaps she had come a little too far?

Suddenly there was an odd popping sound from the bike's engine. It faltered, then picked up again momentarily before faltering again. Then it was slowing, the throaty roar reduced to a sucking sound as the dead engine exerted a braking effect on the bike. Lia pulled in the clutch and coasted on as far as she could, but the machine soon came to a halt. She gave a little cry of dismay. She climbed off and gazed uncomprehendingly at the engine. On an impulse she fiddled with the fuel cap and at last succeeded in opening it. The tank was empty.

At that moment she felt very alone and isolated, and cursed the bad luck that had brought her right back to where she had started. She was in exactly the same position as when she had been swept away by the river all those weeks ago. In the middle of a thick forest completely alone and, worst of all, totally naked.

She glanced about. There were no distinguishing features to the place at all. Her only hope was to find some high ground, as she had on the previous occasion.

Lia set off down the path, abandoning the now useless motorcycle. She guessed there was little chance of accurately retracing her steps through the maze of pathways, but she knew that in order to find safety she must somehow find her way back to the road.

As she walked she thought of Thorkil and his friends. She hoped desperately that they were all right. With any luck Helda and her Bikers would have abandoned the attack when they realised their quarry was no longer there and set off after her. She knew their chances of finding her were virtually zero. They would expect her to have headed for the highway and would be searching miles away. The trouble was that Thorkil would have no idea of her whereabouts either. Her heart sank as she thought of her predicament, lost and miles away from the one she loved.

She walked on for a full hour, searching for something she could recognise, but to her consternation the more she walked the less familiar was the terrain. The trees were strangely shaped, and the flowers were like nothing she had ever seen before. Clearly she had strayed far from the path she had followed on the way in.

Eventually she heard the sound of water and realised how thirsty she was after walking so far. She set off in pursuit of the sound and soon found a small stream. It was clear and inviting and she knelt down and drank gratefully from it, gulping down the cool water. Once she had drunk her fill it occurred to her how hungry she was. It seemed ages since she had eaten the Bikers' stew and her stomach growled. She looked about for something to eat.

An odd shaped tree caught her eye. It was quite tall, but not very broad, its trunk no more than fifteen inches across. Hanging from its upper branches she could see large yellow fruits, that looked as though they might be good to eat. The lower part of the tree was like none she had ever seen before. At even spaces around it were odd protrusions, like stunted branches, each one about ten inches long. They sprang out at an upward pointing angle, and from where she stood they resembled erect penises. She moved closer to the foot of the tree, taking one of the branches in her hand. At this range the resemblance to a male organ was, if anything, heightened, the thick stem opening into a bulbous end. Even the hole in the tip was in place. She ran her hand over the surface of the thing. It was a little rough to the touch, with slight ribbed undulations running across it.

Lia tested the knob for strength and calculated it would support her weight. She placed a foot on it and levered herself up, using another one higher up as a hand hold. She began to climb the tree, stepping from one projection to another and hauling herself ever further up the trunk and closer to the fruits. They hung a good twenty feet above the ground and she clung tightly to the tree as she rose higher and higher.

At last the fruits were within her grasp. She reached up and took one in her hand. Its surface had a furry texture, like a peach, and the flesh felt soft. She twisted it round and it snapped off easily. Then she let it drop, watching as it bounced in the soft grass below. She detached two more in the same manner, then began to descend.

She eased herself down carefully, stepping gingerly from foothold to foothold, taking great care not to scratch her bare flesh. She was no more than five feet up when disaster almost overcame her. The projection on which she was standing suddenly gave way with a loud crack. For a second she was completely off balance. Then she made a grab for a large knob just by her hand and managed just to prevent herself from falling.

Gently she lowered herself to the ground, then leant back against the tree, grateful to be back on terra firma. When she had regained her breath she searched for the piece that had snapped off. It lay in the long grass just a few feet away, and she stooped down to pick it up. The base was green and soft, and she fingered it, fascinated by its phallic shape. It was just like the dildo clients of the Black Cat would make her use, standing her on a table in the middle of the nightclub and making her pleasure herself for the entertainment of the guests.

For a moment a strangely erotic feeling passed through her as she remembered her brazenness. She stroked the object again, and her hand dropped almost subconsciously to her shaven sex, her fingers running lightly over her clitoris. For a few seconds she was in a dreamlike state, the sensation of her fingers on her sex sending a thrill through her body. Then she suddenly realised what she was doing, and the blood rushed to her face. She dropped the thing as if it had suddenly become red hot and, snatching her fingers from her sex, she turned her back on the tree and went over to where the fruits had dropped. She gathered them up, then sat on the ground, deliberately facing away from the tree. She took a tentative bite at one of the fruits, sucking at the juice that leaked from it. It tasted very good; something between a peach and a mango in fruitiness and texture. She began to devour it hungrily. Then the second and third. Soon all that was left were three brown stones.

The afternoon was warm, and Lia felt a drowsiness overcome her. She stretched languidly, enjoying the feel of the soft grass against her bare skin. She lay back, closing her eyes and breathing in the fresh air and the scent of the flowers. She had not intended to doze, but the excitement of the day and the long walk soon got the better of her and she fell into a dreamless sleep.

It was the shadow falling across her face that woke her.

Chapter 5

"Who on earth are you?" a man asked.

It took Lia a few seconds to focus her eyes as she blinked up into the bright sunlight, and slowly became aware that a group of people were staring down at her. There were eight of them. Five men and three women.

They were dressed in a way she had never seen before. The men wore worn jeans, torn and ragged. Two were bare-chested, three wore unbuttoned shirts that flapped in the warm breeze. On their feet were sandals, and their faces were unshaven. The women wore long, shapeless dresses that hung below their knees. These too were shabby and torn in places. All of them, both men and women, wore jewellery of various kinds draped round their necks and wrists, and a few of them had tattoos on their arms and chests and even on their faces.

"I said - who are you?"

Lia turned to face the man, remembering her nudity. She clutched her hands to her breasts and sex in a vain attempt to hide herself from their gazes.

"Speak!"

The man was taller than the rest, and distinguished by the thick gold chain around his neck. On it dangled a jewelled medallion.

"My name is Lia," she said quietly.

"And what are you doing here, in this sacred place?"

"Sacred?"

"Certainly. This is the Tree of Birth. It is at the very heart of the living forest. Your presence in that disgusting state will have angered the spirits."

"Spirits? What spirits?"

"The all-knowing Spirits of the Woods."

Suddenly Lia understood. She had stumbled into a community of New Agers. After the breakdown of law and order many previously established organisations had been changed beyond all recognition. Attendance at conventional churches had been falling for years, and many of the great cathedrals now stood empty and derelict, their windows smashed, their great interiors turned into cardboard cities for the homeless. At the same time many people had begun to turn to alternative religions. Some worshipped ancient gods, others earthly things. Various different cults sprang up, each professing to have discovered the true meaning of life, and for a long time they remained in the cities, trying desperately to recruit people to their causes.

Some attempted to declare parts of the cities safe, preaching peaceful coexistence, but inevitably being wiped out by the tough gangs that roamed the streets. Many others left the urban areas, setting up communes in remote places where they could carry out their rites in peace. For the most part they were ignored by the Bikers, and were allowed to live quietly and practice their religions as long as they stayed away from the highways and service areas which the Biker's considered their own province. Despite the relative poverty in which they lived, the members of these communes began to preach to anyone who would listen of the dawn of a new age. Inevitably they became known as the New Agers.

And now Lia had found them. Or they had found Lia. She glanced from face to face, still clutching her hands to her body, wondering what they wanted with her.

"I - I'm sorry I'm in your wood," she said. "I didn't realise it was sacred."

"But where are your clothes? Don't you realise it is sacrilege to be naked here, except during the most hallowed of services? Why is your body uncovered in such a provocative way?"

"I... I haven't any clothes."

"Look Kieran," said one of the women suddenly, "the fruit. She's been eating the fruit."

The woman pointed at the stones on the ground beside where the confused girl lay. Kieran, the man with the gold chain, picked one of them up and studied it. He turned back to Lia, his eyes wide.

"It's true," he said. "You have been eating the fruits of the tree. Don't you realise that no one is permitted to eat the fruits of the tree?"

"No I didn't know..."

"Wait!" shouted one of the men. "Here is further proof of the little strumpet's evil." He held up the piece of the tree that Lia had snapped off. "She has removed a member from the Tree."

A collective gasp went up from the New Agers as they stared open-mouthed at the object in his hand.

"Give me that," said Kieran, snatching it from him. He took the piece almost reverently, turning it over in his hands. Then he stared again at Lia. "Wicked girl," he shouted. "Look at what you have done to the Tree. This is a profanity that must not go unpunished."

"But it was an accident," insisted Lia. "I didn't know the tree was sacred."

"Ignorance is not an excuse," said Kieran, his eyes wild. "You must make amends to the Tree for what you have done." He turned to the man beside him. "Victor," he said, "she shall be offered to the Tree, and punished there."

"Offered to the Tree?" Victor was dubious.

"Yes. It is the fitting place for her punishment, and it will show her the supreme power of the Tree. Do it!"

Before she fully realised what was happening Lia found her arms grasped and she was hauled to her feet, her hands trapped behind her so that her intimate parts were exposed to the New Agers. She stood confused, while the New Agers began pulling ropes from the bags they carried. As they did so Kieran started muttering some incomprehensible chant.

At a command from him Lia was marched over to the tree, and halted just in front of it.

"Oh Spirit of the Tree," chanted Kieran, "we offer you this strumpet for your pleasure, to make amends for her behaviour. Please accept our offering."

With that Lia found herself being lifted bodily and her legs pulled apart. For a second she was unsure of what they were doing. Then she realised.

They were going to impale her on one of the penis-like protrusions!

She looked down at it with consternation. It was long and thick, and at just the level of her sex. She tried to struggle but the hands that held her were too strong, pushing her onto it. She gave a little gasp as she felt the rough tip brush her sex. Then there were fingers probing at her. Rough, insistent fingers that delved between her legs from behind and stretched the lips of her sex apart. Fingers found her clitoris and teased it into a hard little bud. Fingers that, despite her reluctance, began to have an inevitable effect, causing a warm wetness to flow within her.

They held her suspended, stimulating her until she was lubricated and ready. Then they forced her downwards, so that the phallic tip was pressed hard against the opening of her vagina. Lia gave a cry of dismay and surprise as it slid into her, but despite herself she felt her juices flow even more strongly, coating the rough wood with a sleek lubrication as it penetrated her.

Down and down they pushed her, forcing the wooden knob into her until it could go no further, and her pubic mound was pressed against the trunk of the tree, her nipples brushing the gnarled bark.

As soon as he was certain she was completely impaled, Kieran shouted an order and two stakes were driven into the ground on either side of the tree. Ropes were wound round her ankles and secured to the stakes, leaving her legs spread wide apart. Then they took her hands, wrapping them round the tree and tying her wrists before dragging them up as high as they could and securing them out of her sight.

Lia was helpless, her naked body pressed hard against the tree, her sex filled with the solid wooden cock. All she could move was her head, and she glanced back at Kieran, watching him as he uncoiled a long thin whip. Her stomach turned over as she realised the target she made, her back exposed from neck to ankle, her backside thrust back provocatively by the phallic projection. And yet mixed with the fear was a delicious sense of anticipation, and she felt the muscles of her sex tighten round the wooden cock as she braced herself for the beating.

Swish! Crack!

The whip came down across her beautifully presented rear with a force that drove the breath from her. She closed her eyes and gritted her teeth:

Swish! Crack!

It descended again, this time across her lower legs, cutting into her flesh. She tried to struggle but she was held fast, the movement simply causing her exposed clitoris to rub against the harsh wood, making it swell still further.

Swish! Crack!

This time the leather fell across her back, the hard thong on the end whipping round and catching her breast, leaving a long red stripe that travelled halfway round her body. Lia's skin was bathed in sweat and her body glistened in the afternoon sunlight.

Swish! Crack! Swish! Crack! Swish! Crack!

The whip continued to descend on her punished flesh. But there was a new sensation filling her now, one that made the pain bearable. Pleasurable even. Each blow of the whip rocked her body forward, forcing the wooden shaft to slide back and forth inside her. It was as if the knob and the whip were conspiring together to fuck her, and the sensation to one as lustful as Lia was delicious.

Swish! Crack! Swish! Crack!

Lia struggled to control her feelings as the blows rained down. The pain from the whip was excruciating, but somehow it paled into insignificance compared to the pleasure that ran through her every time she felt the object inside her work its way in and out of her sex. Her nipples had swollen to hard nuts as they were forced against the rough wood, further heightening the tingling lust rising within her.

Swish! Crack! Swish! Crack!

Kieran paused for a second and Lia turned to watch him, still gasping with passion as she hung there. He was drawing his arm right back and she gritted her teeth.

Swish! Crack!

The blow striped across her buttocks with enormous ferocity, raising a spray of sweat as it bit into her reddened flesh.

Kieran lowered the whip but Lia's body continued to writhe. She wanted to stop, but her arousal was too great. Her nakedness, her incredibly erotic position and the punishment had raised her emotions to fever pitch and she drove herself down on the phallus, somehow spurred on by the fact that she was being watched. It was like the scene in the diner weeks before, where she had deliberately brought herself off with the neck of a bottle in front of all the truck drivers. She wanted to be watched; to demonstrate her wantonness to all who wished to see.

Lia's backside was pumping back and forth with urgency as she fucked the tree. A moaning sound escaped her lips and she rammed her hips down harder and harder on the wooden rod, revelling in the sensation of its roughness as it ran back and forth over the walls of her sex. Her clitoris was hard and protruding as she ground it down against the wood, and such was her arousal that a silvery trickle of wetness was running down the trunk of the tree.

"Aah! Aah! Aah!" she shouted.

Then she was coming, the moan turning to a shriek as her passion exploded. She hung, her muscles tensed, her body totally rigid except for her arse, which thrust in jabbing movements as her orgasm flooded her. She threw back her head and cried aloud as the pain and the passion brought her to the most exquisite peak she could imagine, the bondage only serving to increase the sensation as the world seemed to disappear in a blur of pleasure.

Then slowly, by degree, her body began to relax, the breaths coming longer and deeper as the muscles lost their tension. The movements of her backside slowed too and her whole frame slowly sagged, until she hung from the tree like a spent rag, staring shamefacedly round at her audience.

Chapter 6

Lia was brought to her senses by someone undoing the knots that held her wrists. She opened her eyes to see it was Victor. Once he had freed her hands she clung to the trunk while he removed the ropes from her ankles. Only then was she able to separate herself from the tree, easing the phallic object from within her, gasping slightly as it's rough surface slid from her sex.

When it emerged the wooden knob was wet and shiny with her juices. Lia stared down at it shamefacedly, wondering what they must think of her.

Kieran crouched down, examining the surface of the wood, and the trail of wetness that ran down the trunk.

"I think the Spirit has been appeased," he said gravely as he stood up.

"Wait," said Victor suddenly, pointing to the tree. "What's that?"

"What?"

"There, on the end of the thing. It looks like sperm."

"Don't be stupid," said Kieran. "It can't be."

"I tell you it is," Victor insisted. "Just look."

Kieran knelt down and inspected the tree once more. "By the Spirits!" he exclaimed. "It is sperm!"

It was no great surprise to Lia that some spunk had leaked from her. After all, she had already been fucked by both Thorkil and Rico today, and the wooden knob had penetrated her deep.

Kieran rose to his feet. "This is indeed a sign," he said importantly.

"The Tree has shown us the pleasure this young woman brings to it. We must take her back and show the High One."

"You mean the Tree actually released its seed into her?" asked one of the women.

"Of course. I tell you it is a sign from the Spirits."

Lia was flabbergasted by their credulity. How could they possibly believe the sperm had come from the tree? She had heard before of the New Agers' willingness to believe in anything remotely supernatural, but this was ridiculous. And yet they all seemed to accept it as the truth, kneeling by the tree and inspecting the evidence, expressions of wonder pouring from their lips. For a moment she pondered whether she should give them the real explanation, but decided against it, fearing she would appear to be ridiculing Kieran. He obviously had a good deal of power over these people and she was afraid he might make them turn on her if he found out.

Then almost before she knew what was happening her hands were grasped and her wrists tied together behind her back. Her elbows were fastened together, rendering her arms completely helpless, the bonds thrusting her chest forward to accentuate the firmness of her bare breasts.

Once satisfied that Lia's arms were secure, Kieran gave an order and the odd party set off through the forest. A length of rope trailed from Lia's wrists, firmly held by one of the women, who hurried her along, pushing and prodding her if she stumbled. Lia wondered what would befall her. Her freedom had been short-lived indeed, and now she was once more a naked captive, being led into the unknown.

They walked for about fifteen minutes, penetrating deeper and deeper into the woods. The New Agers seemed to know where they were going, but Lia had lost her bearings completely. It seemed impossible she would ever be able to find Thorkil or his Biker friends again.

They crested a rise and the land dropped away in front of them. Lia found herself gazing down into a large clearing, and saw what she assumed was the New Agers' village. It was more of an encampment really, the buildings low and crude, built of wood and mud with thatched roofs. There were about sixty huts altogether, all gathered around a central square where stood a much larger building that dominated the village. Beyond it, right on the edge, was a similarly impressive edifice, resembling a fortress, complete with towers and ramparts.

At the sight of the encampment Lia found herself holding back. It was much larger than she had expected and appeared to be bustling with people. The thought of being led naked amongst so many strangers filled her with dread. But a pinch on her sore bum made her move on, and they began their descent to the village, soon passing the first of the houses, threading their way up a narrow street.

As they made their way between the buildings people came to their doors and stared at Lia. She blushed scarlet at the sight she must make, her breasts jutting conspicuously, her sex hairless and visible, her back and bottom striped with the marks of Kieran's whip.

No sooner had they passed by than the people fell in behind them, whilst others gathered in the square ahead, talking excitedly and pointing at the lovely young girl being led into their midst. Lia looked straight ahead, trying not to catch their eyes. She wished she had some clothes. The humiliation of being naked before all these people was awful, and her face glowed a brighter red than her bottom as she reached the square.

The crowd parted in front of them. Ahead Lia could see a platform about three feet from the ground, with steps up the side. The woman who held the lead shoved her up them, to where there was a single post about four feet high. There was a metal ring set in it which the rope was secured to, leaving her standing with her back to it, staring out over the crowd.

"Legs apart," ordered the woman.

Reluctantly Lia obeyed, aware that her elevated position left her sex totally exposed to the eyes of the onlookers.

"Who is she?"

"Where did they find her?"

"Why is she naked?"

"Look at the brazen hussy, displaying herself like that."

"Someone's been whipping her arse. Just look."

Lia heard the remarks, but tried to block them from her mind. She searched the faces below, hoping for a friendly or sympathetic one, but in vain. Some were leering, others open-mouthed, others licking their lips as they surveyed her naked body. She looked about for Kieran, and spotted him entering the large building at the top of the square. The door was guarded by two women, who wore tiny bikini-like garments of animal skin. Both carried spears.

Lia was left on display in the middle of the square for a full hour. All that time men and women were approaching the dais for a view of her, pointing and making crude and suggestive remarks.

At first she felt nothing but a deep shame, wishing desperately that she was somewhere else, or at least that her breasts and sex were covered. But as time passed something odd began to happen in her mind. Somehow, despite her fears, she began to find her situation strangely arousing. To be placed as she was, bound naked and open before all these people gave her an odd feeling in her belly. She thought back once more to the scene all those weeks ago in the diner, where she had been forced to stand naked on a table before a room full of truck drivers. She thought too of the bottle they had given her, and how delicious it felt when she slipped it inside her. And as these thoughts went through her mind she felt her nipples harden and her sex lips moisten. She was aroused once more, her head filled with thoughts of the men who had fucked her in so many different ways. Try as she might she was unable to suppress the thoughts, even though she was aware that the crowds could see her arousal as they pointed and commented. She closed her eyes tight, trying to control her emotions, praying that Kieran would return soon and release her.

At last she saw the door to the large building open and two women, dressed in the same skimpy outfits as the pair on guard, came out. They crossed the square towards the platform where she was displayed and climbed the steps. The first of them took up a position before her, the cruel tip of her spear placed at Lia's throat so that the hapless captive dared not move an inch. The other woman set about releasing her from the post, and once the rope was undone the spear was removed and she felt another prodding her back, indicating that she was to descend to the square.

The cold metal of the two weapons pressed into her back as they herded her towards the large building. On either side stood the crowd, watching silently as she passed. She had been afraid they might reach out for her body, with her hands pinned as they were, but no attempt was made to touch her and she had the feeling that this was due to the presence of her two guards.

The doors to the building were pulled open by the sentries, and she walked inside. She found herself in a vast chamber, not unlike a church. There were crude wooden benches on either side, laid out in rows, all facing the front. Before them was a large stone which formed a kind of altar, on which was lying a dead rabbit. The blood of the animal was still not dry and trickled slowly down a channel that led to a bowl on the floor, which was already half full of the red, viscous fluid. The sight made Lia shiver.

They led her past the altar and on to the back of the chamber, where there was an archway. She was taken through into a narrow corridor, at the end of which she was ordered to halt outside a door. One of the women knocked and went through, while the other remained at Lia's side, her spear point once more at Lia's throat.

Once the door had closed the guard turned to look at her captive. "Such a pretty little thing," she murmured. She lifted the spear so the metal brushed Lia's cheek.

Lia stayed perfectly still; the point was razor sharp. The guard moved the weapon, sliding the edge down Lia's throat, making the hapless girl tremble. She slid it down her front and over her swelling breasts, just scratching her nipples, the sensation making them harden. The guard smiled and continued to tease them, the edge of the steel sending a tremor through Lia's body.

Then she began to move it lower, prodding gently at her midriff before scraping it ever so lightly down to press gently against her prominent mound. Lia held her breath, aware of what might follow and afraid she would not be able to hold still.

Slowly, inexorably, the blade slid down between her legs and found her clitoris, the threatening edge making her gasp. The sensation on her love bud was extraordinary and Lia felt her wetness flow. The guard went on with her gentle probing, amused at the way the lips of Lia's sex twitched as she teased her.

At last she took her spear away, leaving the tethered girl panting softly. She raised it to Lia's eye level, and let her see the drop of moisture that trickled down the cold steel. Without a word she held it in front of Lia's mouth.

"Clean it off," she ordered quietly.

Lia stuck out her tongue and licked the spear's tip, just as the door opened and the other guard appeared.

"The High One will see you now," she said.

"Who is...?"

"Silence!" snapped the guard. "You will not speak in the High One's presence unless specifically invited to do so. Disobedience of this rule will result in punishment. Do you understand?"

Lia bowed her head. "Yes," she said.

"I am a High Priestess. 'Yes Sereneness' is the correct form of address when you speak to me."

"Yes, Sereneness."

"Now listen. Once inside you will kneel before the High One and await his orders. Do you understand?"

"Yes."

Whack! The second guard swatted the handle of her spear across Lia's backside with a force that made her cry out with pain. "Yes, Sereneness," she mumbled.

The guard brushed Lia's hair from her eyes, gave her a final check over, then stood aside and indicated she was to enter.

The room was lit only by candlelight and Lia blinked in the gloom, unable at first to make anything out. Then her eyes perceived a movement and she saw Kieran. As they came closer to him she realised there was a second man present. He was seated on what could only be described as a throne. It was a large piece of furniture placed on a raised dais. It was covered in wine-red velvet, with gold tassels hanging down from it, and above was a canopy of similar hue.

The man on the throne was about fifty years old, his hair grey and thinning on top. His face was shrouded in a bushy grey beard that hung down almost to his waist. He wore a long multi-coloured robe, and had open sandals on his feet. His face seemed to be painted with some kind of war paint, and on his head he wore a golden spiked crown.

This was the High One.

The guards prodded Lia forward until she was almost underneath the figure, then the blades were placed on her shoulders, forcing her to her knees, obediently before the High One, her eyes cast down, her heart beating fast.

"So this is the mysterious young lady," said the High One. His voice was thin and nasal, not at all the booming voice of authority Lia had been expecting. "Tell me, girl," he went on. "What were you doing in the sacred place? And in that state as well."

"I - I was lost sir," Lia stammered.

Whack! Once again the spear struck Lia's bottom.

"You will refer to the High One as Highness," barked the girl.

"But how did you come to be there?" persisted the High One.

Lia hesitated. The last thing she wanted to do was to admit she was on the run from the Bikers. She feared that if they found out they would hand her over to Helda, and she would be back where she started. She decided to play on their gullibility. After all, if they had believed the spunk on the tree had been supernatural maybe they would believe her.

"I don't understand it, Highness," she said, her eyes cast down. "I suddenly found myself there."

"But why did you steal the fruit?

"I... the tree told me to eat it, Highness."

"Told you?"

"Yes Highness. I heard a voice in my ears bidding me to eat it."

"But you broke a piece from the Tree!"

Lia was thinking fast now. She knew what she was saying was ridiculous, but there was no turning back once she had begun the lies. "It wasn't broken, Highness," she said. "It was a gift. From the tree."

"A gift?"

"Yes Highness."

"For what purpose?"

Lia's face reddened. "For me to... to use, Highness."

There was silence for a few moments, then the High One spoke again. "Show me the piece," he said.

Kieran, who had stood apart listening all this time, stepped forward bearing the piece that Lia had snapped from the tree. It was about ten inches long, with the same ribbed surface and bulbous end as the one on which they had impaled her earlier.

The High One examined the object carefully, turning it over in his hands. Eventually he looked down at the kneeling girl.

"If what you say is true, then this is indeed a miraculous occurrence," he said. He turned to Kieran. "It is possible she was sent for the Solstice Ceremony."

Kieran bowed. "That was what I thought, Highness," he said.

"We shall test her at the New Moon Gathering," said the High One. "Meanwhile I will leave her in the custody of the Priestesses." He addressed the two guards. "You are to impose a regime of the strictest discipline upon her, so she will be ready for the Gathering."

"But you mustn't keep me here," blurted Lia. "I have to find Thorkil."

"Silence!" thundered the woman who stood behind her. "For that outburst you will receive six strokes."

Lia opened her mouth to protest, but catching sight of the glare on her guard's face she closed it again.

"Take her away," said the High One quietly. "And prepare her for the Gathering."

Chapter 7

Lia awoke the next morning to the feel of the sun on her face. She opened her eyes and saw it was shining through a small barred window above her. She tried to sit up, but her hands wouldn't move. She raised her head and looked down at herself.

She was naked and chained to a narrow bed. Her wrists were attached to a ring in the wall behind her, whilst her legs were stretched apart and fixed to similar rings at either side of the foot of the bed. The cell in which she lay was entirely bare apart from the bed. Opposite her was an oak door, with a small triangular window in it.

She couldn't believe her bad luck. After only a few short hours of freedom she was a captive once again. But for what? What had the High One meant about the New Moon Gathering? And the Solstice Ceremony? The New Agers were a complete mystery.

She had learned no more from the guards the night before. By the time they had marched her out of the temple the light was beginning to fade in the sky and the crowd had almost completely dispersed. The women led her down the narrow path between the buildings, their spears at her back. At the edge of the encampment was the building that resembled a fort, guarded by still more of the scantily clad young amazons she now knew to be Priestesses. Her escorts had taken her in through a large gate that opened onto a courtyard. She watched while the gate was secured with a heavy iron lock, then they took her through a door on the far side of the yard, where there was a row of cells. As far as she could tell, all were empty. They led her into the farthest one, locking the door once she was inside, and she remained alone, the only other contact being when they brought her a meal just as darkness was falling. Once she had eaten they chained her to the bed and left her to fall into a troubled sleep, haunted by dreams of Helda stalking her through the woods.

She lay gazing at the ceiling and pondering her fate. So quiet was it that she began to imagine she had been abandoned, and that the entire commune had moved away overnight, leaving her to starve in this bare cell. But at last she heard a noise outside and looked up to see a pair of eyes staring at her through the small window. She squirmed uncomfortably under their gaze, wishing she could cover herself, only too aware of the delightful sight her breasts and sex offered to the onlooker.

The eyes stayed unmoving for about half a minute. Then she heard a key turn in the lock and the door swung open. Standing in the doorway was a man. He looked strangely different from the New Agers. He was dressed in a grey shirt and trousers, clean shaven with none of the body paint or jewellery the others had worn. He stared down at her.

"Now you're a sight for sore eyes, that's for sure," he said, letting his eyes drift over her bare flesh. "It looks like those nutters have come up trumps for once."

He reached out and ran a hand over her breasts, staring into her eyes as he did so. Lia turned away, but he grabbed her chin and made her face him.

"I'm Delgado," he said. "Mr Delgado to you. We have to get to know one another better. We'll be seeing a lot of each other over the next few weeks."

"But what's going to...?" He placed a finger on her lips, silencing her instantly.

"No speaking unless you're spoken to," he said. "I could have you flogged if the Priestesses find out. But I won't tell them just this once. In the meantime..." He stopped speaking suddenly and stared at her face. "Wait a minute..."

"What is it?" she asked, slightly alarmed.

He narrowed his eyes. "Don't I know you from somewhere?"

"I don't think so."

He stared at her for a moment longer, then shook his head. "I dunno," he said, "I don't usually forget a face."

He began undoing her shackles, and soon she was standing beside the bed stretching gratefully. He led her from the cell and down the corridor to a bathroom, where there was a large bath filled with warm water. She wondered where the water had come from, as there was no plumbing that she could see. Nevertheless she was grateful when he nodded to it, and climbed in eagerly. She washed herself all over under his unblinking eyes. It was good to get clean again, but she longed for a little privacy. Clearly she would get none.

When she had dried herself off he motioned to a wooden table in one corner. "Sit on that," he ordered.

Obediently Lia did as she was told, the wooden surface feeling cold and hard against her bare backside. Delgado opened a cupboard and removed a shaving mug and brush. He poured a little water into the mug, then carried it across to her.

"Starting to get a little spiky down there," he said. "We can't have that. Now open your legs wide."

Lia had no choice but to obey. It had been two days since her pubic hair had been shaved and there was indeed a layer of dark stubble there. She hated the idea of being shaved; somehow it made her even more naked and seemed to emphasise her availability. It was like she was making a statement about her promiscuity to all those who saw it.

He began brushing the lather onto her, working all over her pubic mound, then down between her legs, smearing it onto the lips of her sex. She was relieved to discover that the water was warm, and the sensation as he spread it was really quite pleasant. She lay back and closed her eyes, trying not to think of the sight her naked body was presenting to him.

She heard a scraping sound and looked up to see him stropping a razor on a length of leather. It was an old-fashioned cutthroat razor and its blade gleamed as he worked it back and forth.

He began to shave her, letting the blade slide over her skin, carrying with it the small hairs that had sprung through since she'd left the Black Cat. He worked carefully, his fingers touching her intimately.

"Steady now," he said quietly. "I wouldn't want to cut you."

It was all Lia could do to stay still as his hands brushed against her most private and sensitive places. She could feel her clitoris swelling and, with her legs stretched wide, she knew he must be able to see it.

Delgado wielded the razor expertly and was soon finished, much to her relief. He rubbed her over with a damp flannel, replaced the shaving gear in the cupboard, then came back and stood between her legs, gazing down at her. "Yes," he said quietly, "not a bad job at all." He slid his hand down over her sex, allowing his thumb to slide into her slit, and she rewarded him with a groan as it found her love bud.

He smiled and withdrew his hand. "No time for that now," he said. "They'll be expecting you." He took her from the bathroom into another room; some kind of storeroom, with cupboards and drawers all around the walls. "Star sign?" he asked.

"I beg your pardon?"

"Star sign. Sign of the Zodiac. What is it?"

"I don't know. I don't believe in that sort of thing."

"Don't let those nutters out there hear you saying that," he said. "Round here everybody believes. Even me. Now, when were you born?"

"I'm not sure. Nobody ever told me."

"Well, for the sake of these people you'll have to be something." He fished out a small gold chain. "Here you are," he said. "Capricorn. That'll do."

He hung the chain about Lia's neck. There was a pendant hanging from it in the shape of a goat, and he adjusted it so that it nestled between her breasts. The metal felt cold on her skin and she shivered slightly, not liking the ridiculous trinket at all.

He fastened a second fine gold chain around her waist, and another around her ankle. Somehow the jewellery seemed cheap and made her feel rather tarty. At last he was satisfied with her appearance and, after running a brush through her hair a few times, led her from the room. He produced a pair of handcuffs and fastened her wrists behind her back, then he opened a door and took her out into the sunlight.

The courtyard was empty apart from two guards who stood by the main gate. Delgado marched her smartly across to a door, and when they reached it he rapped loudly, then opened it, pushing her inside and closing it without entering with her.

Lia looked about. She was in a small hallway with a single exit opposite the door through which she had been pushed. She hesitated for a second. Then since there was nowhere else to go she pushed the door open and stepped through.

Chapter 8

The room Lia entered was large, with a high ceiling supported by thick wooden pillars. The walls were covered with murals depicting strange scenes. Creatures that were half man and half beast were in unfamiliar landscapes. Some of the pictures seemed to have no form to them at all, just meaningless swirls and splashes of colour. In addition to the murals were the statues, some in recesses high in the walls, others freestanding about the room. Many were of odd, ugly beings that stood on two legs, great phalluses projecting from their groins. Others were of winged beasts with long curved talons, some of them bearing the body of some hapless woodland creature.

The only furniture was a series of divans that stood around the walls, draped with brightly coloured cloths that had the coarseness of a fabric woven by hand.

Lia stood glancing round uncertainly. There was another door on the far side, but her instincts told her to remain where she was.

She had been waiting for a number of minutes before she heard the sound of someone approaching. Her body stiffened. Her months with the Bikers had taught her to take a submissive stance when in such situations, and although she was unable to place her hands behind her head because of the cuffs, she was still able to straighten her back and place her legs apart before the door opened.

The beautiful young women who entered were dressed in the same manner as the ones who had escorted her on the previous day. Only the colour of their skimpy outfits varied; some being almost white whilst others were a much darker hue. There was no sign of the cruel spears. They made their way to the divans, where they draped themselves, some giggling as they pointed at her.

The one in the lightest coloured outfit went to a divan in the centre, close to where Lia stood. She reclined gracefully on it, then beckoned Lia closer. "The High One tells me that you were found at the Tree of Birth. Is this true?"

"Yes, Sereneness."

"And is it also true that you had sex with the Tree?"

One of the other girls giggled again, but a withering look from Lia's interrogator silenced her at once.

"Well, is it?"

"Yes, Sereneness."

"And the Tree actually released male seed into you?"

"So they said, Sereneness."

"Where do you come from?"

"I don't know, Sereneness." The answer was at least in part truthful, since Lia had been brought up an orphan and knew no details of her past. In any case, the woman seemed to accept it without question.

"What do you know of the Spirits of the Forest?" she asked.

"Nothing, Sereneness."

"Yet you were in the Sacred Place?"

"I - I don't know how I got there."

The interrogation went on for some time, with Lia professing ignorance at every possible opportunity. Eventually the woman seemed to accept that she would learn no more from her young captive, and began to talk about the New Agers themselves.

"I am Karla," she said. "I am the Senior Priestess of our colony. We escaped from the darkness of the city after the High One had a vision telling him of the Spirits of the Forest and urging him to come out here and serve them. Once in the forest the Spirits guided him to the Tree of Birth, which is the most sacred place on earth. So we built our village nearby, erected the temple and began to worship. In return the Spirits have been kind to us and we have not gone hungry. Now, it seems, we have been sent you. The High One believes it is for the Solstice Ceremony, but first you must pass the test of the New Moon Gathering. The High One told you this, I believe?"

"Yes, Sereneness."

"The Gathering is not for three weeks. Until then you will remain here in the Fortress Retreat with the Priestesses. It is important that you understand who we are."

"Yes, Sereneness."

"The people of this community are dedicated to the service of the Spirits. It is also necessary, however, for them to build and dig and sow in order to sustain life. The Spirits are generous, but must be assisted in their work by the labour of the people. In order to ensure that the true meaning of the Temple is not obscured, therefore, they appoint us Priestesses to offer praise and prayer. We carry spears, mainly for ceremonial reasons, but our chief duty is to the praise of the Spirits and the High One. For this reason we live here in the Fortress Retreat, and only venture out to guard the Temple and to join in the services there. Do you understand?"

"Yes, Sereneness."

"No man from the commune is permitted inside the Fortress, and we are forbidden all contact with males during our five year tenure. Yes, I know Delgado is allowed inside, but he is not one of us, and even he is not allowed here, in the Inner Sanctum. Delgado has his reasons for wanting to hide from the outside world, and we do not question them."

"Yes, Sereneness."

"While you are in the Fortress you will carry out duties that will keep you occupied. Once a day you will attend the worship in the Temple, as the people will wish to see you. At all times you are to be obedient to the Priestesses and to the High One. Is that understood?"

"Yes, Sereneness."

"Good. Now, I believe Shuna has something to report from yesterday."

Two of them rose from their divans, and Lia felt a sinking feeling as she recognised the Priestesses who had escorted her the day before.

"Speak, Shuna," said Karla.

Shuna was the girl who had gone ahead into the High One's reception room first, leaving Lia and her companion Lisbet outside. She frowned at Lia as she began to speak. "This person has already transgressed," she said.

"Then it is your duty to speak, Shuna. How has she transgressed?" Shuna frowned again. Lia wondered why she seemed so reluctant to tell Karla of her misdemeanour. She had shown no affinity towards her up to now.

"She... she spoke out of turn to the High One," said Shuna at last.

"And did the High One order a punishment?"

"Yes."

"Go on."

"He... he has ordered six strokes."

"I see." Karla turned to Lia. "Is this true?"

Lia hung her head. "Yes, Sereneness," she muttered.

"Then the sentence must be carried out. On both of you."

Lia looked up in surprise.

"You see," Karla was smiling as she explained, "here at the commune we believe guilt must be shared. We are duty bound to report any misdemeanours we come across, but in doing so we may appear to be sitting in judgement. So the punishment is meted out to the accuser, as well as the accused. And since Shuna was given the duty of reporting the punishment, then she must receive the same."

Lia shook her head. These people had the strangest customs she had ever encountered. No wonder Shuna had been so reluctant to report her.

"Right," said Karla, "let me see your backside, young lady."

Lia hesitated for a moment.

"Your behind," said Karla sharply. "Show it to me."

Slowly Lia turned around.

"Bend forward."

She obeyed, displaying her bottom to the Priestesses. It was still red from her punishment the day before, with cruel marks across both cheeks.

"Hmm," mused Karla. "It seems you've been pretty well punished there already. I think a thong across those lovely white thighs might be in order."

The words sent a chill through Lia, and with it an odd sense of excitement as she thought about what was intended.

"Stand up and turn around," said Karla. She looked round at the young Priestesses. "Now who shall have the honour of carrying out the punishment? Someone new, I think." She pointed to a youngster, who was sitting on the outside of the gathering. "Stand up, Charlotte," she said.

The girl rose to her feet. She looked about nineteen years old. She was slim and beautiful with firm breasts that bulged out over the top of her bikini, and rounded hips. Her hair was dark, and hung down over her shoulders, framing her pretty face beautifully. Lia noted that the colour of her outfit was dark brown. The colour of each Priestess's clothes seemed to be an indication of her status, demonstrating that Charlotte was some kind of novice. Karla's costume was almost white, and Shuna's and Lisbet's were a light tan.

Charlotte stepped forward, her pretty brown eyes wide. Lia could see from her demeanour that she was nervous. She wondered if it was the first time she had been asked to mete out a punishment, and guessed it probably was.

"Fetch the thong," ordered Karla.

Charlotte crossed the room to a cabinet on the wall, and opened it. Lia caught a glimpse of an array of canes, whips and manacles inside, the sight of which sent a wicked thrill through her. Charlotte reached in and withdrew something from a shelf, then closed the cabinet again. As she returned, Lia saw she held a small leather strap about a foot long. She handed it to Karla, who slapped it onto her palm a couple of times, it making a loud cracking sound as she did so.

Karla motioned to Lia to approach the central divan. It was low, but it rose at one end into a headrest which was thick and padded. "Stand with your back to it," she ordered.

Obediently Lia took up the position. The eyes of all the Priestesses were on her. Shuna, standing close, seemed unmoved at having to witness the punishment that in a few minutes she too would be receiving. The one who appeared the most nervous was Charlotte.

"Bend back over the divan," said Karla.

Lia shuffled backwards until she felt the leather headrest against her bum. Then she slowly leant back. It was slightly awkward, since her hands were still manacled, but she eased herself down until she was lying with her head on the flat surface of the couch, her backside raised high on the headrest. Without waiting for the inevitable order she spread her legs wide. She knew she offered a perfect target for the punishment, her inner thighs exposed, as was her sex.

"Mmm, very nice," said Karla, as she gazed down at the girl. "Come forward, Charlotte, and feel how soft her flesh is."

The girl approached nervously, and Karla took her hand, placing it flat on the smooth flesh of Lia's inner thigh. Still holding her wrist, she guided Charlotte's hand up to the naked captive's sex.

"Feel for her love bud," she said. "Make it hard. I want to see if she really responds to punishment in the way they say she does."

Gingerly Charlotte ran her fingers over Lia's clitoris. Lia gritted her teeth, trying hard not to respond to this intimate touch, but she was unable to prevent a gasp escaping her lips as Charlotte took her love bud between finger and thumb and began to toy with it. The girl was inexperienced and her caresses were rather fumbling, but still it aroused a spark of lust in Lia as she fought hard to stay still.

She looked up and caught the eye of the girl who was caressing her. To her surprise she realised the girl's nervousness had disappeared. In its place Charlotte wore an expression of longing as she gazed down at Lia's nude body, laid out so submissively before her. For a second their eyes met, and at that moment something seemed to pass between them. Suddenly Lia realised she wanted the girl, with a passion she had never felt towards another female before. She wanted to strip off the girl's skimpy garment, to caress those lovely young breasts and taste her virgin honeypot. The connection lasted only a few seconds, and then Charlotte turned her eyes away in embarrassment. Lia, having dropped her guard, gave a small moan as the fingers continued to work on her.

"That's enough," Karla said suddenly. Lia looked up, wondering if she had seen the glance between her and Charlotte. "She's nice and ready," went on

Karla. "Begin the punishment."

Charlotte accepted the thong from Karla and stood between Lia's legs. She bit her lower lip, and Lia could sense this was going to be difficult for her.

Charlotte raised the thong, and Lia shut her eyes.

Crack!

The leather caught Lia's inner thigh, making a sound that rang about the room. Lia jumped as the pain hit her, then lay still again.

Crack!

This time her other thigh received the blow, the leather cutting into the flesh, leaving a deep red stripe that ran almost to her sex.

Crack!

Lia cried out as the leather snapped down onto her sensitive skin. The pain was excruciating, and with it came that familiar burn in her sex that was so hard for her to understand. She gazed up between her breasts and open thighs at Charlotte, who was raising the thong yet again, and a spasm of lust ran through her as she once again imagined the girl naked and in her embrace.

Crack!

The fourth blow fell, stinging Lia dreadfully. She could see that despite her apparent feelings Charlotte was not sparing her. Perhaps it was because she realised the perverse pleasure Lia received from being beaten. She hoped that was the case.

Crack!

Again Lia shook as the leather bit. The blow was higher up her thigh, and the tip of the thong snapped against her sex lips. Lia felt moisture on her thighs and realised to her chagrin that the beating had released her juices. Her face glowed at this betrayal of her desires.

Crack!

The final blow descended, placing another weal across the whiteness of Lia's flesh, and once again she allowed herself a cry of pain. Then she felt the softness of Charlotte's hand on her flesh again, stroking over the marks she had placed there. Lia could see there were tears in the girl's eyes, and she gave her a small smile of encouragement.

"Note that her bud is still hard," said Karla, and Lia squirmed as she felt Charlotte touch her there once more. "Pull apart her lips and show us."

Charlotte put the thong on the couch, then placing a hand on either side, eased Lia's sex lips apart. Lia's face grew redder still as they all saw the evidence of her arousal.

"Hmm," said Karla. "An interesting reaction. Almost unique. This really is a most unusual young lady. Now," she turned to Shuna, "your turn I think."

Chapter 9

During the next few days Lia's life developed something of a routine in the New Agers' camp. Every morning she would be woken by Delgado, who would supervise her toilet, after which she would be laid out on the table while he shaved her sex. This was a duty he continued to carry out, despite her protests that she could do it herself. He would always take the opportunity to excite her clitoris as he worked, enjoying watching the arousal it awakened in his captive.

Once he had finished she would be allowed into the Priestesses' inner sanctum where she would be given breakfast in a dining room with the women, though always on a separate table.

Her daily duties were varied. Some days she would be put to work cleaning and polishing in the Priestesses' living quarters. On others she would work in the kitchens or the washroom, where she would labour alongside the more junior Priestesses. Occasionally she would encounter Charlotte. She longed to talk to the girl, but the young Priestess was clearly uneasy in her presence. And besides, Lia was forbidden to speak unless spoken to.

Every evening her hands were cuffed behind her back and she would be led through the village to the temple. She always hated the walk. The people would line the streets and watch her as she passed, their eyes roving over her naked form. Once inside the temple it was no better. The Priestesses had placed the wooden phallus on a small shelf set into a plinth about three feet up on the temple wall. Lia would be made to stand on the plinth beside it, her hands stretched above her and fastened to a ring in the wall. Here she would stay in full view of the worshippers while the strange rituals of the New Agers were acted out. Throughout the service she would stare straight ahead, trying to ignore the eyes upon her. Some of the stares of the congregation were disdainful, others wondering. Not a few of the men would eye her lovely breasts and sex with undisguised lust. This she found very disconcerting, as it kindled emotions within her, and she would have to fight to avoid giving evidence of her own arousal to the watchers.

During this period she had no sexual contact of any kind, being carefully supervised when she was working and manacled to the bed at night to prevent her masturbating. This was deprival indeed in one so lascivious as Lia, and at night, when left alone with her fantasies, she would imagine Charlotte's body pressed against hers and her sex would ache with desire.

A week went by, then another and still the routine continued. The time spent with her beloved Thorkil seemed an age away. She wondered if he was still searching for her. And if Helda was. She shuddered to imagine what it would be like if the woman caught her again, and her dreams were still haunted by the face of the Black Cat's proprietor.

Then one day there came an abrupt change to the pattern of her life.

Towards evening Lia was led as usual from her workplace, and stood in the main chamber waiting for the handcuffs to be attached for the walk to the temple. But instead she was led to the door to the courtyard, where Delgado was waiting for her.

"Follow me," he ordered, and led her to the cell block and into the bathroom.

"Two baths today," he said, and indicated the steaming tub. Lia climbed in obediently. As usual he did not allow her to lie down in the water, but made her stand while she washed, allowing him to watch every intimate detail of her ablutions. Normally he was silent with her, only speaking to issue orders, but tonight he began to talk as she washed.

"You know what's special about tonight, don't you?"

"No Sir." He had insisted from early on that she refer to him as Sir.

"It's the New Moon."

Lia felt a strange coldness at the words. Ever since the New Moon Gathering had been first mentioned by the High One the thought of it preyed on her mind. She knew it marked some sort of test, but she was unsure for what. Now she heard the words again a sense of foreboding overcame her.

"You know what it means, don't you?"

"No Sir."

"It means that you're going to be found out. And when they discover that you violated their precious Tree of Birth they're not going to be very pleased."

"I - I don't know what you mean."

"Oh yes you do. I heard about the spunk on their precious Tree of Birth."

"Spunk?"

"Don't play the innocent with me, young lady. You know what I'm talking about."

"It was some kind of message from the Spirits. That's what they said."

"Then they're even stupider than I thought. Trees don't produce spunk. They're just wood and sap. If there was spunk on that tree it must have come from inside your cunt."

"But they said..."

"I know what they said. They're just a bunch of gullible idiots. If someone in bright clothes with enough jewellery told them the world was going to end tomorrow they'd believe them."

Lia considered his words. They were probably true. "But why do they believe these things?" she asked.

"Because they want to believe. Because they want to bring some kind of meaning into their silly little lives. That's why. And that's why they're not going to be very pleased with you tonight when you give your performance."

"Performance?"

"That's right."

Lia felt an odd feeling in her belly. She looked at him nervously. "What will I have to do?" she asked.

"Screw yourself."

For a moment Lia was not sure whether this was some kind of insulting dismissal, but it had not been said with any vehemence. "I beg your pardon?"

"They're going to make you screw yourself. With that wooden cock you broke off that damned tree. And they're going to expect to see spunk. But they won't, will they?"

Lia did not reply.

"Will they?" he persisted.

"No Sir," she muttered.

"I thought not. So who'd been fucking you before your encounter with the tree?"

"A Biker. Called Rico."

"A Biker's girl, eh? You must have really had the hots for him to wander about starkers like that."

"I'm not Rico's girl."

"Even better. He shares you round does he?" Lia turned away. Delgado grinned, enjoying her discomfort. "Still, it doesn't solve tonight's little problem, does it?"

"No Sir."

"Of course, there is one solution."

She looked at him. He was still smiling, his eyes roving over her young body. She blushed hotly. There could be no doubting what he meant.

"Right," he said suddenly, "time we shaved that pretty little cunt of yours. Can't have it looking scruffy when so many people are going to get a look at it. On the table with you now."

Lia stepped out of the bath and lay across the wooden surface, opening her legs for him.

Delgado began to shave her, working the lather over her flesh then setting to work with his razor. As he held the lips of her sex apart his thumb found her clitoris, making her moan quietly as he gently teased it.

"Well then," he said, "what about it?"

"About what Sir?"

"You know."

Lia looked at him, her face scarlet. She knew, of course. And she also knew that she had no choice. The New Agers would expect to see spunk on the wooden dildo, as they had before, and there was only one place to get it from. She took a deep breath.

"Will you fuck me please, Sir?" she asked quietly.

"I beg your pardon?" He was wiping the last of the foam from her hairless mound, his fingers gently caressing her love bud as he did so.

"Will you fuck me please?" she repeated.

"Me? Fuck you?"

"Yes please, Sir."

He dropped the cloth, but his fingers continued to stroke her sex. "You'd like that, wouldn't you?"

A small whimper escaped from Lia's lips as he penetrated her with his index finger. He had never fingered her so blatantly before, normally contenting himself with a few strokes as he shaved her. Being deprived of sex for so long had made her extremely horny; the constant nakedness seemed to arouse her, despite the fact that she hated it so much, and being shaved as she was made her doubly so.

"I said you'd like that, wouldn't you?" he repeated.

"Mmm," she mumbled, her eyes closed.

Whack! He brought his hand down hard on her inner thigh, making her jump with pain and surprise.

"Yes Sir," he said.

"Y-yes Sir," she stammered.

"That's better. You're enjoying this, aren't you?"

"Yes Sir."

"Tell me."

"I'm enjoying having your fingers in me."

"In where?"

"I'm enjoying having your fingers in my cunt."

"And what do you want?"

"I want you to fuck me."

It was true. She did desperately want him to fuck her. His touch had brought on her arousal almost at once, and she longed to feel a hard, thick cock inside her. He swivelled his fingers and she rewarded him with a groan of pure lust as she thrust her hips up at him.

"Would you like to suck my cock too?" he asked suddenly.

"Yes please Sir." There was an unmistakable eagerness in Lia's voice as she replied.

"On your knees."

Lia scrambled off the table, feeling a trickle of moisture escape onto her thigh as he withdrew his fingers. She dropped to her knees before him, gazing expectantly up into his face.

"Suck me," he ordered.

Lia reached for his fly, fumbling with his belt, then yanking down his zip. She reached into his pants, her hand closing around his stiff rod, which sprang to attention as she released it, jutting out at her face. She didn't hesitate for a moment. Opening her mouth she took him inside, sucking greedily at his great member. She wanted him badly now. More than she would have thought possible. Her pussy was soaking as she imagined his firm cock inside her and she licked as her sex lips convulsed with the thought of it.

Suddenly he grabbed her hair and pulled her face away from him. She gazed up at him, saliva coating her chin. "On your hands and knees," he ordered.

Lia obeyed at once, turning her back on him and crouching down, her lovely backside thrust up at him, her legs spread apart so that her pussy was open and available to him. He reached down to her, running his fingers over her anus and sliding them into her vagina.

"Oh!" She gave a little cry of delight as she felt him probe her wetness once more. She widened her legs in an unambiguous gesture of submission. Then he was kneeling behind her, and she felt the hard tip of his cock brush against her bum. She pushed back at it, willing him to penetrate her.

"Guide me inside," he said.

Lia reached back gratefully, her fingers closing about his massive knob. She pulled on it gently, giving a little start as it touched the wet lips of her pussy. She pressed it against herself, rocking back towards him. For a second her flesh resisted. Then he was inside and sliding deeper and deeper into her dripping sex.

"Ahhh," she groaned, ecstatic with the sensation of his mighty organ filling her completely. She was almost beside herself with pleasure. It didn't matter that she was being forced to kneel on the floor of a bathroom while he screwed her. All that mattered at that moment was that she was being fucked. That her lascivious desires were being satisfied by the cock inside her.

"Mmm..." She gave a low moan as he began to move, working his hips back and forth, sliding his erection back until it was halfway out, its shaft glistening with her juices, before ramming it home once more, almost toppling her over such was the force of his thrusts.

Delgado gripped her hips in his hands as he fucked her, holding her tight while he thrust his cock into her. Lia tried to respond to his rhythm, pushing back as he pressed forward, willing him even deeper. Her body shook with his onslaught, her dangling breasts quivering as she struggled to maintain her balance. Her head was down, her hair hanging over her face, little cries escaping from her lips. She knew she couldn't hold back for much longer, such was the exquisite pleasure Delgado's cock was bringing her.

She didn't have to. With a grunt Delgado shot his load into her, making her come instantly, her cries echoing round the bathroom as she milked the spunk from his balls. Wave after wave of pleasure washed over her as her orgasm burst. Still he didn't stop, his hips pumping back and forth, depositing the last of his seed deep into her. Then he was slowing, his breathing becoming more easy as the passion ebbed away.

At last he was still, sliding his cock from her as she slumped forward onto the floor, gasping for breath. He flung the flannel down beside her. "Better wipe yourself clean," he said. "But make sure you leave some in there."

Ten minutes later a manacled Lia was being led from the fortress by the Priestesses whilst Delgado watched from across the courtyard. Once the gate was closed he turned away, back into his own quarters. As soon as he was safely inside he turned the key in the door, then crossed to a writing desk. He opened a drawer and extracted a glossy document which he laid on the desk. It was in the format of a magazine, and across the cover were emblazoned the words *The Black Cat. Prospectus*. He opened it to a well-thumbed page, to a full-spread photograph of Lia. She was naked, leaning back on a table, her legs spread wide so that her sex was open. Delgado studied the picture for a few moments, then gave a slight smile and closed the magazine, slipping it back into the drawer.

Chapter 10

There seemed to be more New Agers about than ever as Lia was led down the street. All around were people, dressed in their most brightly coloured clothes and festooned with jewellery. It made the naked girl feel very conspicuous indeed, especially since her hands were trapped behind her, leaving her no means at all of covering her body.

The crowd was in festive mood, dancing and singing and taking long swigs from the jugs of liquor that many of them carried. Clearly the New Moon Gathering was a time of revelry, and the air was full of laughter and gaiety.

Lia made her way through the people with her escort, her head down, trying to blot from her mind the comments of the people as they passed. She had expected to be led to the temple as usual, but clearly today's plan was a different one. Just before they reached the square the Priestesses turned away down a side alley. It was a route with which Lia was not familiar, and her puzzlement deepened as she saw that it led out of the village and into the wood. They led her along a path lined on either side by New Agers. As they passed the people fell in behind them, so that Lia found herself leading an ever lengthening procession through the trees.

The route twisted and turned for some distance before eventually opening out into a clearing. In the centre a bonfire had been lit, and Lia could make out the shapes of people as they danced round it. The area was lit by flaming torches stuck in the ground, so that despite the gathering gloom, it was bright as day in the centre of the circle.

A cheer went up as Lia appeared and the crowd ran to greet her, laughing and pointing. There were many faces Lia had not seen before and she guessed that more than one village was gathering for the festival. As usual the people were in awe of the Priestesses and stood apart as they approached, ogling the girl they brought with them.

In the centre of the circle, close to the bonfire, was a wooden platform, to which Lia was being led. She sighed as she saw it; these people seemed to want to put her on display whilst what she wanted was to hide away from their hungry eyes. She longed to be able to cover herself. To hide her modesty, like other girls could. But she possessed no clothes, and with nobody willing to give her any she was condemned to display her nakedness to anyone who wanted to see it.

Sure enough, Shuna and Lisbet led her up the steps onto the platform. She was reminded of the public whipping she had received from Miss Goram all that time back at the depot. She had been caught sucking off a truck driver in his cab while his companion fucked her from behind, and had been punished for her wantonness in front of the whole depot. Now it was not punishment she faced, but something equally humiliating, and it was with an air of foreboding that she stepped onto the platform.

Projecting from the floor was a thick post with a cross-member attached at the top, at shoulder height. Shuna released Lia's hands, then she and Lisbet took a wrist each and pulled them out to the sides, lashing them to the cross-member so that she stood with arms outstretched, gazing down at the crowd. They left her feet free, but Shuna made her spread them apart before they left her there. Lia leaned back against the post, resigning herself to a long evening.

The frolics continued, with Lia left to watch, standing like some pagan idol, staring down at the revellers below. There seemed no particular ritual or format; they would run round and round the fire, shrieking with laughter before collapsing at the foot of the stage, gazing up at the captive. Many shouted lewd remarks at her, but Lia remained silent. As time went on she began to become aware of a tension in the air. Everybody seemed expectant, their eyes drawn to the path down which she had been brought. There was no doubt they were waiting for something, and Lia was not at all sure she was in a hurry to find out what it was.

Suddenly a shout went up and fingers pointed along the track. Lia squinted in the direction they were indicating, but at first could see nothing. Then far in the distance she discerned a light. It was almost night now, and the light appeared like a flickering beacon among the trees.

The people went silent and began to make their way towards the edge of the clearing. The mood was eerie. They did not speak, their actions almost trancelike as they drifted towards the source of the light. In a few minutes Lia found herself alone, apart from Shuna and Lisbet, who remained at the foot of the stage.

There was a strange sound, almost like a low moaning, and Lia glanced about, trying to locate its source. Then she realised it was the crowd. They were chanting some kind of mantra in low voices, the sound carrying through the air like a droning hum that grew louder as she listened. The light was much closer, and as she strained her eyes she could discern figures moving through the trees towards them. And all the time the strange chant continued to echo through the wood.

It took quite some minutes for the meandering light to reach the clearing. Long before that Lia had lost sight of it amongst the flaming torches of the waiting crowd. She knew it was close though, as with every minute the volume of the chanting increased. The people were almost shouting when

43

finally she saw them begin to part, allowing the new arrivals to pass between them.

The procession, when Lia eventually saw it, was a small one. In the lead was one of the Priestesses bearing the flaming torch that had been visible from so far away. Behind her marched Kieran, who carried before him a cushion on which lay the wooden phallus. Lia eyed the object with consternation; it signalled that she was soon to become the centre of attention.

Behind Kieran were four more Priestesses, bearing a sedan chair, and on the chair sat the High One. He wore a gold robe, with the crown on his head, and he was waving lazily to the crowd, who held up their hands to him, still yelling their strange chant. Behind the High One marched Karla, her head held high, staring straight ahead, apparently oblivious to the throng around her.

The strange procession made its way to the centre of the clearing and finally drew to a halt in front of the stage. The High One's chair was lowered to the ground and the others flanked themselves on either side of him. The High One raised a hand, and suddenly the people were silent. Slowly he rose to his feet and raised his hands skywards.

"See!" he shouted. "The new moon. The Spirits are favouring us!"

A cheer erupted, and looking up with the rest, Lia was just able to discern the thin sliver of the new moon, low down on the horizon. She turned her attention back to the crowd, who were all staring in silent wonder into the sky. They remained watching it for another five minutes. Then Lia saw the High One turn to Karla and nod. She began to chant in some strange language that Lia did not understand, and after every sentence the crowd would reply with something equally incomprehensible.

The service went on for a long time. Lia looked on in bewilderment as they chanted, sang and danced about the fire. To her none of it seemed to make sense, but one thing was for certain. At the centre of attention was the phallus, which had been deposited at the feet of the High One.

All of a sudden Lia became aware that the atmosphere had changed. Once again an air of expectancy seemed to prevail and she realised with a shock that all eyes were turned in her direction. She looked down to see that Karla had picked up the cushion on which rested the phallus, and was making her way up the steps of the stage where Lia was tied, with Shuna and Lisbet behind her.

Karla moved round in front of Lia, with the other two Priestesses on either side. She placed the cushion on the floor at Lia's feet, then stood facing the young captive. Once again Lia was painfully aware of the flowing robes that covered the Priestesses' bodies, while she was forced to remain naked, her firm breasts jutting conspicuously.

Karla seemed to sense Lia's thoughts, for as the crowd watched she stretched out a hand and cupped Lia's left breast, running her palm over the nipple and feeling it stiffen beneath her touch. She slid her fingers down Lia's smooth skin, pausing to stroke her hairless mound before delving into her most private place. Lia gave a moan as the woman's fingers found her clitoris, and she realised her sex was already wet. The bondage and the exposure among all these people had seen to that. She was apprehensive, afraid that Karla would delve too deep, and discover the fluid Delgado had deposited in her earlier that evening.

"Is she ready?" called the High One from below.

In answer Karla held up her fingers. They were shiny and wet, and glistened in the firelight. A murmur of assent rose up from the crowd. Karla held out her fingers to Lia. For a second she hesitated, then licked them clean. Once again the crowd rumbled its approval.

Shuna and Lisbet undid the ropes that held Lia's wrists and she was free, rubbing the red marks where her bonds had been. As soon as they had released her the three Priestesses retreated back down the steps, leaving the naked girl alone on the platform.

"Now must you show us whether you are indeed blessed by the Spirits," said the High One in his shrill, whining voice. "In the Sacred Place it is said that you managed to evoke the very seed of the Tree of Birth with your lustful ways. Now we wait to see if you are indeed the one we await."

Lia stood silent as he continued to speak. She wasn't listening now. Her eyes were on the thick, curving length of wood that lay at her feet, and she felt a warmth rise in her tummy as she contemplated what they were about to make her do.

"Pick up the piece of the Sacred Tree," called the High One.

Lia took a deep breath, then stooped and took hold of the thick shaft. She straightened up again, holding it in her hand.

"Now use it," said the High One. "Let the Spirit of the Tree of Birth penetrate you and take his pleasure in you. Give yourself to him!"

There was complete silence now as the expectant crowd stood watching Lia. She glanced down at the object in her hand, running her fingers over its rough surface, feeling the bulbous end. She raised it to her mouth and licked the tip, letting her saliva dribble down its length. Lia was aroused. Standing exposed and naked with the stiff phallus in her hand she suddenly wanted it inside her. And she wanted the crowd to watch as well. Just what perverse trait of her character gave her such lascivious desires she did not know. Most girls of her age would be overcome with shame, hiding themselves away and refusing to perform such an outrageous act. But Lia wanted to do it. She wanted to expose herself to the crowd. And most of all she wanted to feel the stout object inside her, to satisfy her incorrigible desires.

The tip was shiny and wet now, and she rubbed it against her erect nipples, wiping saliva across her creamy flesh. Then she was moving it lower, down towards her hot, wet sex. She spread her legs, bending her knees slightly and leaning back against the post. The pink of her sex was open, the wetness within visible to the crowd, who jostled for position below the stage, their eyes wide with anticipation.

It touched her clitoris. She whimpered quietly at the sensation, rubbing the rough surface back and forth over her erect love bud. Holding the knob in her right hand, her left went to her breast, feeling for the nipple, which puckered and hardened at once. She squeezed gently between finger and thumb, all the time stimulating herself below. Her body was on fire with lust and all pretence of decorum discarded as she abandoned herself to her pleasures.

She cast her eye over the crowd, imagining the men's cocks hardening in their pants at the sight of her, and she felt a drop of love juice escape onto her thigh.

"By the Spirits, look at that!"

"She's really horny!"

"I wish it was me, not that phallus!"

Lia heard the comments, a new thrill running through her as she imagined the sight she was making, standing naked in the firelight and caressing her body openly. She began to move the phallus downwards, sliding it over the open lips of her sex until the tip was rubbing against the entrance to her vagina. She turned it, so it was pointing upwards towards its goal. Then, with a final glance out over her audience, she began to press.

She was so wet her flesh offered no resistance at all, and with a cry she felt the rough wood penetrate her. She pushed again, sliding it deeper and deeper, revelling in the feel of the wood as it forced apart the walls of her sex and filled her completely. She let go of it, her latent exhibitionism dominating her desires as she stood, her hands behind her head, her hips thrust forward, allowing the crowd to see how intimately she was pierced by the wooden length. Its dark shaft projected from her cunt, and she began to gyrate her hips in a lewd and silent dance. Reaching down she took hold of it again. Slowly, her eyes fixed on the crowd, she began to move it, working it gently back and forth inside her, holding it only in thumb and forefinger as she delicately pleasured herself.

"Mmm..." she moaned softly as the wood rubbed over her sensitive flesh. The sensation was incredible, and her body was aglow with lust. She began moving it faster, working it in and out with a new urgency, her other hand once more caressing her breasts. She was almost shaking with desire, trying desperately to hold herself back, to prolong the pleasure the dildo was giving her.

"Ahh!" A sudden wave of lust ran through her, and with it all self-control was lost. She took hold of the wooden shaft in her fist and began ramming it hard into her vagina, every thrust bringing a hoarse grunt from her throat. Lia was a picture of wantonness, standing as she was, her legs apart and bent at the knees as she worked the sturdy wooden object in and out, grasping it in her fist as if she were a man wanking his own cock. Her thighs were spattered with her juices, and more ran down the shaft of the phallus onto her fingers.

The wetness caused a sucking sound as she worked it in and out, and her breasts bounced with every stroke, much to the delight of the onlookers.

Lia could feel her orgasm coming close, and her hand began to work back and forth even harder. Her teeth were gritted, her body tense, her eyes tight shut.

Then it hit her.

"Ahh! Ahh! Ahh!" She threw back her head and screamed as waves of pleasure washed over her, the roughness of the wood taking her to new heights with every stroke. The orgasm was loud, blatant and public, but Lia didn't care. She was slumped back against the post, ramming the thick phallus into her vagina for all she was worth, crying aloud, her long dark hair waving back and forth as she lost herself in bliss. She wanted the sensations to go on forever, but already her motions were slowing and she began to return to reality. Gasping for breath she let her head drop, watching her fingers as they pumped the glistening phallus back and forth, the urgency gone now, but the enjoyment still there. Gradually though her actions subsided until the only movement was the twitching of her sex lips. She remained motionless, staring down at the wooden object that projected from her sex. Then, slowly, she began to pull it out, easing it gently with both hands. As it emerged the crowd could see the wetness that coated it, shining in the firelight.

With a gasp she finally pulled it free. She held it close to her face, inspecting it, then gave a little cry of triumph and held it up to the crowd.

The end was sticky with sperm!

Chapter 11

Lia's life at the New Agers' commune changed considerably after the New Moon Ceremony. No longer was she kept in a cell, but allowed to sleep in the Priestess' inner sanctum, where she was provided with a room of her own. She was still chained to the bed at night, but during the day she was free to wander about the sanctum and even in the courtyard if she wished, though she tended to avoid anywhere outside the domain of the Priestesses, for fear of meeting Delgado. She felt that the incident before the Gathering had somehow given him a hold over her, and his knowing looks when they met were something she found unnerving.

During the days, therefore, she tended to keep to her room, emerging only for meals. These were now sumptuous affairs, served to her by the junior Priestesses at a high table in the dining room. It seemed that no luxury was too good for her now, and she was bathed in the sweetest smelling perfumes, usually attended by a young Priestess.

Despite these luxuries, though, she was still aware of being a prisoner, and of being allowed little or no free will. Requests to be allowed out of the fortress were always greeted with a polite refusal, and even her trips to the temple ceased. All the time she continued to be forbidden clothes, despite her desperate entreaties. Her life became a strange one, in which she felt totally alone despite being surrounded by fellow human beings. She would often wonder about Thorkil, and whether he was still searching for her. She was desperate to get word to him of where she was, but could think of no way to do so. In order to contact him she would have to get word to an outsider, and there was nobody.

Except Delgado.

The dilemma tormented her. She deeply mistrusted the man, and feared the power he held over her. But he was the only one to see the antics of the New Agers for what they were. Just silly superstitions. She knew that if there was any chance at all of getting word to Thorkil it must be through him. So at last, after much soul-searching, she resolved to approach him.

It was not as easy as all that. Whilst she had not been forbidden contact with him, she knew that spending any length of time in his presence might arouse suspicion. To be completely safe she had to speak to him in secret. And to do that she had to choose her moment carefully.

She took her chance in the middle of the day, when most of the Priestesses were at the temple and she knew she was certain to find him in his room. Once the place was quiet she slipped out of her room and made her way to the main anteroom, which she was relieved to find deserted. From there she found her way to the outer door, which led into the courtyard. She opened it a crack and peered out. There was nobody in sight. She slipped into the open, and as she hoped the fortress was completely silent. Up on the turrets she could see the figures of the duty guards, but they were facing out towards the village, so she was able to cross to the cell block unnoticed. She tiptoed up to Delgado's door and knocked softly.

"Who is it?"

"It's me, Sir."

"Who?"

"Lia, Sir."

There was a pause, then footsteps and the sound of a bolt being slipped back. Delgado's face appeared. He eyed her up and down. "What is it?"

"May I come inside please Sir?"

He hesitated, and for a moment she thought he was going to refuse. Then he gave a shrug and opened the door wider, beckoning for her to enter. She stepped inside. It was simply furnished with a low bed, a dresser and one or two chairs. The walls were decorated with girlie calendar shots and motorcycle posters. He beckoned to her to sit on one of the hard chairs and she did so gingerly, the wood feeling cold and unyielding against her bare backside after the sumptuousness of the Priestesses' furnishings. He did not sit, but remained standing, looking down at her.

"To what do I owe the pleasure of this little visit?" he asked.

"I..." Now she was there Lia found it hard to begin. "I need your help."

"My help? But surely you're living the life of Riley now that the nutters

48

think you're some kind of messiah?"

"I'm a prisoner here. You know that."

"In a gilded cage."

"I want you to get a message to someone."

"A message? How?"

"There must be some way; you're free to come and go as you please."

"Yes, but it's miles to the nearest civilisation."

"But there must be a way," she insisted.

"I might be able to get hold of a horse for a few hours. But what if I did? How am I going to find this friend of yours?"

"You have to try. It's my only hope."

"Who is this friend of yours?"

"He's a Biker. His name is Thorkil."

Delgado gave a low whistle. "Thorkil, eh? Of Depot 29?"

"You've heard of him?"

"Certainly I've heard of him. He's a pretty high-powered chap. You mean you're his girl?"

Lia nodded.

"Hmm, Thorkil eh?" he mused. "It wouldn't be easy. I'd be taking a hell of a risk."

"I - I'd make it worth your while," said Lia quietly.

"How?"

"Thorkil has money."

Delgado snorted. "Money! What do I want with money? Besides, how could I be sure you'd keep your word?"

"But I would."

Delgado shook his head. "No, I want something in advance."

Lia stared long and hard at him, then dropped her eyes. "You can do anything you want with me," she said.

Delgado grinned. "Nice idea," he said. "But I had my heart set on more forbidden fruit."

"What do you mean?"

"Well," he said, "you know that gorgeous young Priestess? The little brunette?"

Lia looked at him in surprise. "You mean Charlotte?"

"That's her. Gorgeous little filly. I'd love to see her out of that bikini of hers."

"You want to have sex with Charlotte?"

"That's the idea."

Lia was silent for a moment. She thought about the request. Ever since her punishment she had held the girl in some affection. The thought of Delgado getting his hands on the young virgin appalled her. Besides, she knew it would destroy her position as a Priestess, and despite her scepticism she knew that such an occurrence would destroy Charlotte's life.

"I'm sorry, I can't do that," she said. "It wouldn't be fair."

"Then there's no deal," he replied.

For a moment Lia was devastated. Her last chance to find Thorkil seemed doomed. Then a thought struck her.

"There is one thing I can do," she said.

"Tell me."

"Well, you say you'd like to see Charlotte naked."

"That's right."

"What... what if I had her punished?"

"How?"

"What if I had her bare bum thrashed for you?"

A slow grin began to cross Delgado's face. "Hmm," he said. "That sounds interesting. But how would you arrange it?"

"The other day, during their fast, I saw her take a bread roll from the kitchen. That's punishable by six strokes."

"For you and for her, I understand."

Lia looked away. "Yes."

"The only trouble is that watching the two of you get thrashed will make me pretty horny."

Lia blushed. "My offer still stands," she muttered.

Delgado was silent for a moment. "All right," he said at last. "When can you do it?"

"Tomorrow morning," she replied. "Be at the door to the sanctuary at eleven. They'll all be still at prayer then, before the lunchtime service, so I can smuggle you in."

"You've got a deal," he said.

Lia rose to her feet. "I'd better go."

He walked to the door with her. As she reached for the handle he grabbed her hand, twisting her arm and pressing her against the wall. He reached up with his other hand and grasped her breast, squeezing roughly.

"Now you won't let me down, will you?" he growled.

"No Sir," whispered Lia.

He reached down between her legs, and she gasped as he penetrated her with two fingers.

"I'm rather looking forward to having you again," he said, twisting his digits inside her so that she gasped once more. "Are you looking forward to it too?"

"I... yes Sir," she said, trying desperately to control her body as it responded to his touch.

He worked his fingers back and forth a few times, enjoying the reaction he received from his wanton young companion. Then he withdrew and reached for the door handle. "Till tomorrow then," he said.

Once he had closed the door behind her he slipped the bolt across, and once again a grin crossed his face. He went to the dresser and pulled out the Black

Cat prospectus, turning as always to the page where Lia's naked charms were displayed. He thought about what she had asked of him. Silly little bitch. She was playing right into his hands, and finally giving him an opportunity to escape from this dismal place.

Delgado was not at the New Agers' commune by choice. Like Lia he was an exile from the Bikers. From Helda, in fact. Three years before he had been employed at the Black Cat. He had a good job, well paid, and had every opportunity of becoming a Biker himself one day. But he had been too greedy, too impatient.

He began filching money from the takings. Small amounts at first, but then as he became bolder, larger sums. They set a trap and caught him red-handed. His escape was a desperate one, diving through a window and stealing a motorcycle. Ever since he had been holed up here, where he felt safe from discovery.

But now he had the chance to return. He knew Helda was seeking Lia still, he had heard of it weeks before during a rare visit to a service area. If he could be the one to hand her over then surely it would put him back in favour with her. Possibly even gain him a reward. He smiled slyly as he stared down at Lia's photo. He would restore her to the Bikers, all right. But not to Thorkil.

Chapter 12

The next morning, after breakfast, the Priestesses retired to their room for private prayer, as they did every day. Lia waited until all was quiet in the sanctuary, then went to the door. Delgado was waiting by the cell block opposite, and he crossed the yard quickly.

Lia put a finger to her lips. "Don't make a sound," she whispered. She led him into the main anteroom, and he looked about at the decorations with interest. It was the first time he had ever seen the inside of the place. He knew to be there was a risk, but the thought of seeing the lovely Charlotte punished made it worthwhile.

In one corner of the room was a large cupboard, in which brooms and cleaning equipment were kept. Lia opened it. The door had holes cut into it, about an inch in diameter and positioned at eye level. Their purpose was for ventilation, but they were ideal spy holes. "In there," she whispered.

Suddenly he grabbed her, pulling her to him and placing his lips over hers. He held her close, his tongue probing her mouth while his fingers found her bare sex. Lia tried to resist but he was too strong. His fingers slid into her and she felt herself go weak, her body responding in a manner that was at odds with her mind.

He kissed her long and hard, enjoying the feel of her bare flesh pressed against him, and the way her cunt pulsated round his fingers. When he released her she was panting slightly, her legs weak.

"Just a little appetiser, my dear," he said, leering. Then he stepped into the cupboard and allowed her to shut the door.

It was barely five minutes later that the Priestesses filed in through the door and took their places. Some lay on their couches, whilst others gathered in small groups, chatting quietly together. This was a rest period for them before the service began at noon, and they generally spent it here. In the corner Lia spotted Charlotte talking to another of the novices. She seemed deeply involved in the conversation, but Lia noticed she was darting frequent glances across at her as she always did. Lia took a deep breath. She was not looking forward to what she had to do next.

"Please, Sereneness," she said, her voice unnaturally loud, so that conversations ceased and eyes turned in her direction.

"What is it?"

"I'm sorry to have to tell you this, Sereneness, but I have to report a misdemeanour."

"A misdemeanour? Tell me."

"During the fast the other day I saw a Priestess take a bread roll from the kitchen and eat it."

As she spoke she saw Charlotte's eyes open wide and her face grow pale.

"Who was it?" asked Karla.

"It... it was Charlotte."

"Charlotte!" There was an air of strict authority in Karla's voice as she barked the name.

"Yes Sister?" Charlotte's voice, in contrast, was small and meek.

"Is this true, Charlotte?"

"It was only a little roll," she protested. "I'm sorry, Sister. I was hungry. I..."

"Silence!" snapped Karla. "Did you eat during the fast or not?"

"I did, Sister."

"And you know the punishment?"

"Yes Sister."

"What is it?"

"Six strokes, Sister."

"Then it seems we have two young ladies to punish." She turned to Lia. "I'm sure you haven't forgotten our custom of chastising both the miscreant and the accuser."

"No, Sereneness."

"Step out into the middle, Charlotte."

Slowly, hesitatingly, the girl crept across the room to stand beside Lia. She stopped in front of her, staring uncomprehendingly into her eyes, then turned to face Karla.

Lia felt desperately sorry for the girl. She wished there was some other way, but she could see none. She had to get word to Thorkil, and if this was the only way then so be it. Still her heart went out to the young Priestess. She resolved to hide her own fear as best she could, in the hope that it would give the girl some encouragement.

"Fetch the belt, and two pairs of cuffs," ordered Karla. "We haven't had a proper double punishment for ages. Now Charlotte, remove your clothes."

The girl stared fearfully around the room, obviously deeply embarrassed at the suggestion. Lia knew how she felt. She was constantly aware of her own nudity, and still found it difficult to come to terms with baring her breasts and sex to complete strangers.

Slowly the girl reached for the knot that secured her top. She fumbled with it for a few seconds, then pulled it undone. The skimpy garment fell away, leaving her naked to the waist. Charlotte's breasts were exquisite. Not too large, but rounded and full, the small brown nipples slightly oval in shape. Lia was surprised to feel an intense thrill as she contemplated sucking them.

Charlotte's hands were at her waist. The brief skirt was also held up with a single knot and it came undone easily. For a second the girl held it, then she let it fall away, leaving her totally nude. Lia found herself transfixed by the bush of dark hair at the girl's crotch and by the thick pink lips between her legs. Her body was tanned a rich brown except where the bikini had been, and the patches of white flesh around her breasts and sex only served to accentuate her nakedness. She thought of Delgado, watching from his hiding place. From where she stood Charlotte offered him a full-frontal view of her lovely body.

"Bring the belt," ordered Karla.

Lisbet stepped forward. In her hands she held a thick brown belt, all around the surface of which were brass rings. Lia was puzzled by it. It seemed too thick and unwieldy to be used as an instrument of punishment, and she was soon to discover that the belt had a different purpose altogether.

"Stand them face to face."

Lia felt her arms grabbed from behind and she was turned to face Charlotte. At the same time Shuna grasped Charlotte's arms. The two naked girls stood barely six inches apart, staring into each others' eyes.

The woman who had been holding Lia stepped back and Lisbet took her place. She wrapped the belt about Lia's waist just above her bottom, then handed the two ends to Shuna, who pulled, and Lia found herself pressed hard against Charlotte.

The two young women were forced together in the most intimate manner. Their breasts were squashed firmly against one another, so that Lia could feel Charlotte's nipples against her own, and the girl's pubic hair rubbing against her bare mound. The closeness was extremely arousing to Lia, and even before the punishment began she knew she would have difficulty disguising her passions.

Behind Charlotte the Priestess was slipping the end of the belt through the buckle and pulling it tight. Lia felt the breath squeezed out of her lungs, the leather biting into her flesh, but despite this she was still unable to suppress the eroticism that being forced against Charlotte's warm toned body kindled inside her. The sensation of the girl's flesh on hers was extraordinarily arousing and her senses were alive with the closeness of her fellow miscreant.

Once the belt had been cinched tight she felt Shuna reach for her hands, pulling them round behind Charlotte's back. Then a pair of cuffs were snapped on her wrists and she realised that the short chain between them had been attached to one of the brass rings on the belt, so that her hands were trapped behind the girl. Moments later Charlotte's wrists were fastened behind Lia in a similar manner.

Lia glanced across the room to a large mirror that hung below one of the murals. It reflected the pair of them beautifully and she guessed that was precisely its purpose. The sight it offered was both thrilling and frightening. The two girls were as one, their slim bodies squeezed together, their legs intertwined, their bare backsides presented perfectly for the punishment to come. They looked like two naked lovers embracing, the golden brown of Charlotte's flesh a sharp contrast to Lia's much fairer tone.

She pressed her cheek against her companion's. The girl smelt of lavender water, but beneath that was a stronger odour and she felt a pang of excitement as she realised it was the scent of arousal. It excited her greatly to realise that Charlotte too was turned on by their closeness. She wanted to kiss the girl, but feared that the two of them would receive an even worse punishment for such a misdemeanour.

She watched as Shuna and Lisbet both selected canes from the cabinet. The canes were made of bamboo, and gave a swishing sound as the two women made practice strokes through the air. Charlotte heard the sound too, and a faint whimpering escaped her lips as she anticipated what was to come. Lia hugged her, trying to alleviate her trembling.

The two Priestesses took up their positions behind the naked girls, and Lia shivered as she felt the cane tapping her backside.

"Begin," said Karla.

Swish! Whack!

The two canes struck with perfect synchronisation on the buttocks so beautifully presented. Lia felt a sting of pain as the weapon bit into her, whilst her hips thrust forward against Charlotte's in an almost sexual gesture as the girl reacted to the stroke across her own bottom.

Swish! Whack!

Once more it was impossible to distinguish between the sounds as the twin canes lashed their hapless victims. Charlotte gave a cry of pain, whilst Lia bit her lip, determined not to betray how much the punishment was hurting.

Swish! Whack!

Again the two girls slammed together as the canes descended. The stroke stung terribly, but the proximity of Charlotte's body, and the knowledge that she too was being punished was intensely erotic for Lia. Her nipples were in direct contact with Charlotte's and she felt them pucker to hardness as a wave of passion swept through her. She realised Charlotte's were responding in a similar manner, the sensation of her hard buds against her own doubling the sensation.

Swish! Whack!

With every jolt Lia could feel her own lascivious passion rising. She glanced at the mirror. Charlotte's behind was bright red, with four obvious stripes crisscrossing it and she knew her own must look the same. She imagined the effect the sight must be having on Delgado, and the thought of the fucking that must inevitably follow her punishment sent a wave of lust through her. She could feel the wetness of Charlotte's tears on her cheek, but at the same time she could feel the pressure of her pubic mound as she pressed against her own in an unambiguous gesture of sexual arousal.

Swish! Whack!

Shuna and Lisbet were striking with a deadly accuracy, their blows perfectly in time, and the two naked girls made an extraordinary sight, writhing in a dance that suggested carnality rather than pain. They were both bathed in sweat and glistened as they hugged tightly together.

Swish! Whack!

The stroke cut into Lia's arse and Charlotte's cry of pain confirmed that her final blow had been equally vicious. But the main sensation Lia felt now was desire for the young woman she held in her arms. Despite her smarting bum, or possibly because of it, she wanted nothing more than to possess the girl, to taste the juices she could feel flowing, to suck those succulent nipples and bring her to orgasm under her fingers.

"Release them."

Lia felt hands on her wrists, undoing the cuffs. The belt was undone, and for a few seconds the two of them stood hugging one another, though no longer joined. Then Charlotte broke away and collapsed onto one of the divans, her head buried in her hands. Lia stood where she was, resisting the temptation to rub her stinging backside, staring across at the cupboard where Delgado was concealed.

For a moment there was silence. Then Karla spoke.

"Right, Sisters, time we were at the temple." She stooped where Charlotte lay. "You are excused today's service," she said quietly. "When you're feeling better, perhaps you will assist the preparation of lunch."

The Priestesses filed out of the room, leaving Lia alone with Charlotte and the concealed Delgado.

Chapter 13

The moment the door closed Lia knelt down beside Charlotte. Gently she ran her fingers over the girl's bottom, feeling the cruel red stripes, aware that her own bore similar marks.

"I'm sorry," she whispered. "Believe me I had a very good reason to do what I did. Are you all right?"

Charlotte turned her face toward Lia. She stared quizzically at her. "But why me?"

Lia kissed her on the cheek. "It had to be you, that's all." She continued to run her hands over the firm flesh of Charlotte's bottom, trying to ease the pain of the beating. "Does that feel any better?" she asked, then leaned over the girl and kissed her scorched bottom, planting delicate kisses on both cheeks. Charlotte lay where she was, but Lia sensed she liked the feel of her lips on her skin. Charlotte lay with her legs slightly parted, and Lia could see the pink lips of her sex, like some precious flower bud, not yet opened but showing promise of blooming into something extraordinarily lovely. Tentatively she stroked them. Charlotte gave a little start, but said nothing.

Lia looked across at the cupboard, where she knew Delgado was watching her every move. She imagined how hard his cock must be as he observed them both, and she felt a thrill as she remembered her promise to give him relief once she was able to release him.

Charlotte gave a little moan, and Lia felt a dampness seep onto her fingers. She looked at the lovely young virgin. She had her eyes closed and her mouth slightly open. Her bottom was starting to move slightly in time to Lia's fingers.

"Roll over onto your back," Lia whispered.

The girl hesitated for a moment, lifting her head from the couch and gazing guiltily about. She rolled over, revealing her firm breasts and dark thatch to both Lia and the secret watcher. The sight of her succulent globes was too tempting for Lia to resist. She lowered her head over them, taking one nipple between her lips and sucking. She felt it grow harder in her mouth and flicked her tongue back and forth over it, enjoying its rubbery texture. Her hand crept down over Charlotte's belly, seeking out her furry little love nest.

"No," murmured Charlotte as Lia's fingers found her slit. But her protest turned into a little sigh of pleasure as Lia touched her clitoris and rolled it between her finger and thumb.

Lia licked and sucked at Charlotte's breast, squeezing the other with her left hand. Her right hand remained buried between the open legs of the young Priestess. The girl was panting slightly, her hips moving back and forth as she responded instinctively to the touches. Lia was overcome with a desire to taste the girl's cunt. She knew Delgado was watching her every movement, and what a sight it would make to see her adoring the sex of another girl, but

56

she didn't care. What mattered now was Charlotte's pleasure.

She took her lips from Charlotte's teat. It stood out hard, glistening with saliva. She kissed the girl, their tongues licking one another as her hand went on teasing the little love bud. Then she began sliding her head downwards, pausing to kiss both breasts and her belly before staring directly into the wet succulence of her sex.

She lapped at Charlotte's hard little clitoris, eliciting a gasp from the supine girl. Then she was sucking, clutching Charlotte's hips as the girl writhed beneath her. Her fingers resumed their work on Charlotte's button as her tongue moved lower, savouring the taste of the girl's juices, flowing freely now. She delved her tongue deep into Charlotte's vagina, making her cry aloud with delight. Charlotte was panting with excitement, and Lia sensed she was close to an orgasm. She licked still deeper, tasting the girl's arousal, holding tightly to the girl's hips as she thrust her cunt hard into Lia's face, urging her on.

All of a sudden Charlotte stiffened. She cried aloud as her orgasm overcame her, her limbs completely rigid, her legs wide apart, her sex pressed hard against the mouth that fed on it so exquisitely. She gave a little mewing sound, her breasts vibrating slightly as she arched her body. Then she was moving again, thrusting herself lewdly against her lover's face, her breath coming in harsh grunts as she allowed her climax to flow through her. Lia clung doggedly to her, drinking her juices as they flowed, intent on giving her all the pleasure she had to give.

With a sigh Charlotte relaxed, sinking back down onto the couch, her eyes closed. Lia straightened up and Charlotte blinked her eyes open, as if awakening from a deep sleep. She stared at Lia for a second, then gave a little cry, folding one arm across her breasts and covering her sex with the other. She shrank back into the couch.

"What is it?" asked Lia gently.

"We... we shouldn't have done that."

"Why not?"

"Because it's wrong."

"You enjoyed it didn't you?"

"No. Well, yes but..."

"But what?" Lia moved closer to the girl, stroking her hair. "You're so beautiful," she said, "I just couldn't resist it."

"But what if someone were to find out?"

"Who could possibly find out? There's only the two of us." Actually there were three, but there was no way Delgado would admit to having been in the inner sanctum.

"I must go." The girl rose to her feet and began searching for her clothes. "I must get to the kitchen before the Sisters return."

She made for the door, but Lia took her by the arm, swinging her round to face her. She took the girl in her arms, holding her close, their bare breasts pressed together. She kissed her, feeding her tongue into the girl's mouth. For a second Charlotte was stiff with resistance, but then she relaxed into Lia's embrace, returning the kiss with equal enthusiasm.

At last Lia pulled away, gazing into her young lover's eyes. "OK now?"

"Yes," said the girl.

"Back to the kitchen then," said Lia, patting her bottom.

The girl went to the door. Just before she went out she turned to Lia. "I loved that," she said.

"I know," said Lia. Then the girl was gone.

Lia stood gazing at the empty doorway, her heart still beating strongly with the passion of lovemaking. The girl was the most beautiful thing she had ever seen, and she longed to have her for her own. So she resolved that, if her escape was successful, she would return one day to make Charlotte a Biker's girl too.

Her thoughts returned to the present, and to unfinished business. It was time to let Delgado out of the cupboard. She crossed to it, and paused there for a second, gripping the handle. A thrill passed through her as the reality of the situation hit her. She was about to be fucked, whether she liked it or not. With mild surprise she realised how much she wanted it, and there was a genuine eagerness as she opened the door.

Delgado emerged, his pants undone and his cock sticking up stiff as a ramrod.

"Jeez, I'm horny," he gasped. "I'm going to fuck the arse off you now, you sexy little slut."

"Not here..." Lia began, but he was already pushing her to her knees and forcing his swollen cock between her lips. His urgency was infectious, and Lia knew she was anxious to have him inside her. She sucked hungrily, his groin grinding against her flushed face.

"On the couch," he barked suddenly.

Delgado wasted no time on foreplay, thrusting his cock into her and pumping away aggressively. Lia bit her lip to stop herself crying aloud. She had never experienced such urgency. He fucked her for all he was worth, the couch creaking under his powerful thrusts, his hands mauling her breasts. Suddenly a hoarse cry escaped his lips and he was coming, filling her with hot spunk and triggering her own shuddering orgasm as he did so. She held him close, her hips pumping against his as they both savoured the release of the moment. Then they collapsed onto the couch, both limp and exhausted.

It was Delgado who moved first, pulling out roughly and stuffing his cock into his pants. "Back to my room," he said. "I haven't finished with you yet." With a sharp whack on the backside he propelled her to the door.

Chapter 14

The days leading up to the Solstice Ceremony were busy ones in the colony. Talk seemed to be of nothing else and there was a tangible air of excitement amongst the Priestesses as they prepared special dishes and cleaned and sewed their ceremonial garments. Lia was almost ignored amid the frenzied preparations, a fact that she rather welcomed. She had something else to occupy her.

Since the punishment Delgado's demands on her had been almost nonstop, and she had lost count of the number of times he pulled her into his room and fucked her on the bed, the floor, the chair, wherever took his fancy.

She acceded to his demands without complaint, for all the time she knew the day of her escape was drawing closer. Her only fear was that the Priestesses would find out about their sessions, but all seemed too preoccupied with the ceremony, and scarcely a day passed without Lia finding herself bent across Delgado's bed with his cock jammed into her.

Then one morning, as she knelt on the floor of his room, wiping spunk from her chin after sucking him off, he told her his plan.

"It'll be during the Solstice Ceremony," he said. "It's the ideal time, because you'll be out of this bloody fortress. I've got word to a couple of friends of mine, and they'll be helping."

"What's going to happen?" asked Lia.

Delgado ignored the question at first, taking a candle from a drawer and tossing it to her.

"Use that," he said shortly.

Lia examined the object. It was thick and smooth, about nine inches long. She ran her fingers along its length, stroking it as she would an erect penis. As she did so she felt the familiar heat kindle in her belly. She knew what she had to do with it. She was growing used to Delgado's tastes by now.

She stretched herself out on the floor and spread her legs. Reaching down she worked two fingers into her slit, easing the lips apart. Then, her eyes fixed on her companion, she positioned the tip of the candle against the entrance to her vagina and pressed. It slid in easily, gliding over the walls of her sex and disappearing deep into her love hole, until only the very end was visible, protruding between her soft, pink nether lips.

"How does that feel?" asked Delgado.

"Mmmm..." she murmured.

"Wank yourself," he ordered.

Lia began to gently masturbate, working the candle in and out as she lay on the floor, staring up at him.

"T-tell me about the plan," she muttered through clenched teeth.

"It's simple really." Delgado sat in the chair opposite her, his cock still stiff, massaging it slowly as he watched her. "We're setting up a small diversion. A couple of sticks of dynamite."

"You're not going to hurt anyone?" For a second Lia ceased her movements, a look of alarm crossing her face.

He kicked her foot. "Get on with it."

Lia's hand began to move once more, working the candle in and out of her sex with a steady rhythm. The phallic object was having its desired effect, and he could see her backside begin to grind as her arousal grew.

"Don't worry," he said, "nobody's going to get hurt. The explosions will be some distance from the ceremony. Play with your tits."

Obediently Lia took one hand from the candle and cupped a breast. She began to caress them, squeezing and kneading, making the nipples stand erect whilst frigging herself with the makeshift dildo. To Delgado she made a delightful sight, stretched out on the floor of his room, naked and alive with passion. He began to wank in earnest, his own desires fully rekindled.

"You... you still haven't... oh! You still haven't explained..."

Delgado smiled; he liked it when she began to lose control. He had never known a girl so easily turned on, and such a slave to her desires. And to his.

"The explosions will be to the east of the site, about a quarter of a mile away. The idea is that when they go off everyone will be looking in that direction, while we ride in from the west."

"Ride?"

"Lift your arse off the floor. Thrust your cunt at me. Offer it to me. That's right."

Lia did as she was told, planting her feet on the floor and raising her bottom, supported by her shoulders, working the candle in and out with urgency, her breath coming in short gasps.

"Now tell me you're a slut."

"I... oh!"

"Tell me."

"I-I'm a slut," she gasped through clenched teeth.

"And a fucking little whore."

"I'm a fucking little... oh!" Lia gave a sudden lurch as a spasm of pleasure ran through her. "I'm a fucking little whore!"

Delgado grinned again. He had risen to his feet and stood looking down at the girl as she pleasured herself, his fist working his foreskin back and forth.

"I think I'm coming," she whimpered.

"Don't. Not yet. You'll come when I give permission."

"But I can't..." Lia's body was on fire and she desperately needed the release of an orgasm, but she knew she must obey. She must hold herself back.

"Wh-what are you going to be... ahh... what are you going to be riding?" She tried to turn her mind back to the subject of the rescue, in order to take her thoughts off the pleasure that was threatening to consume her.

"Horses, of course. You've just got to be ready for us to pick you up."

"But I've never ridden a..." Her voice trailed off into a moan of bliss, her hand working the candle eagerly into her vagina, her breasts quivering with every stroke. "I've never ridden a horse."

"Don't worry, I'll do the riding. Tell me how you feel."

"L-like I'm being fucked."

"And you like being fucked, don't you?"

"I... yes."

"Say it."

"I like being... oh! I like being fucked. Oh please..."

Delgado moved closer until he was standing between her legs, gazing down at the girl as she masturbated frenziedly, her head rocking from side to side. "Look at me."

She gazed up at his thick cock. The sight of him wanking over her sent a new thrill through her and she almost screamed with frustration. She had to come soon or go mad.

"At the Solstice, listen for the explosions," he said. "Understand?"

"Yes."

"Don't stop now," he said; her motions had slowed in an effort to regain control.

"But I can't... oh, I can't stop myself." Lia was bathed in sweat, her breasts shining in the light from the window as they trembled.

"Don't look towards the explosions when you hear them. Look the other way. That's where we'll be coming from. Have you got that?"

"Yes. Look the other way. Oh please let me come!"

"Come when I do," he said.

She looked up at him, watching anxiously as he worked his foreskin back and forth. She wanted to scream such was her arousal and she watched his face for some sign of his climax.

All of a sudden a great spurt of semen erupted from his cock. It flew in a high arc and splashed hot and sticky onto her upturned face. Her orgasm exploded too, her mouth open in a silent scream. Another spurt spat from him, carefully aimed to land inside her mouth. She swallowed it greedily, offering her face for more as she writhed beneath him.

He continued to shoot his thick come onto her. As his passion ebbed so it spewed less far, hitting her breasts and belly until the last of it dribbled down onto her pussy lips, the sight of his rampant organ covering her with spunk spurring her to new heights of passion.

He tucked his cock back into his trousers and stood gazing down at her, lying on her back, her naked skin covered with sticky sperm that dribbled from her face and breasts. Her vagina was still filled by the candle, although she had released it as she lay panting beneath him.

"You'd better have a bath before those Priestesses see you," he said.

Chapter 15

The day of the Solstice dawned warm and bright, and Lia found herself caught up in the preparations for the ceremony. There were hampers to pack and things to be carried here and there. It was as if they were preparing for some enormous party. Dozens of people came to collect bags and boxes and other strange objects that Lia guessed were part of the ceremony.

All the time there was no sign of Delgado. The Priestesses tut-tutted at his absence at such a time, and there was no doubt that had he shown his face he would have received a severe ticking off. But he didn't appear, and Lia's excitement grew as she thought of where he was and what he was planning. Who could say how soon she would be back with Thorkil?

At last all seemed ready, and Lia was summoned to Karla.

"Time to prepare you for the ceremony," she said. "After all, you will be a very important guest."

Shuna and Lisbet led Lia away. There were some parts of the building that were still forbidden to the young captive, and she was surprised to find herself taken through a door that had previously always remained locked. They led her down a corridor, and at the end was another door, through which she was taken. The room was small. Some kind of storeroom, she guessed. There was a table, on which lay a collar with a long metal chain, like a dog's lead. The collar was about two inches wide, fastened by a pair of buckles, one above the other. Around its circumference were shiny studs, as well as a ring to which the lead was attached. Beside the collar lay a pair of clamps, small with sharp metal teeth, and they too had chains attached, although these were smaller and more delicate than the one on the collar.

Lia stood uncomplaining as the collar was fitted. It was snug, just tight enough not to restrict her breathing. Shuna fiddled with the adjustment for some time before being satisfied, the lead dangling down Lia's front. Shuna then surprised Lia by cupping and caressing her breasts. Apart from her encounter with Charlotte none of the Priestesses had ever made a sexual advance to her, and she gave a gasp as the woman rolled her nipples between her fingers so that they responded immediately, hardening to firm buds. Shuna lifted the two clamps from the table, and with a shock Lia realised what they were for. She shrank back from the Priestess, but her hands were suddenly snatched behind her back and there was a click as a pair of cuffs closed about her wrists. She watched in trepidation as Shuna squeezed one clamp, making the jaws open, then extended it towards Lia's breasts.

"Oh!" Lia gave a little cry of pain as the cruel teeth closed over her erect nipple, biting deep into the flesh so that for a second she feared they might pierce her. She gritted her teeth as the second one was fastened to her other nipple. The pain was excruciating, bringing tears to her eyes. But with it came a sensuous pleasure she had barely experienced before, strangely arousing, and she felt a hot flush pass through her body as the clamps bit into her flesh.

Shuna stood back to admire her handiwork, cupping Lia's breasts in her palms and tugging at the chains to ensure they were secure. Lia had to bite her lip to prevent herself from crying out. Shuna made a sign to Lisbet and she took hold of the lead that dangled between Lia's breasts. She gave a little tug, indicating that Lia was to follow her from the room. They led her back through the anteroom into the courtyard. There the Priestesses were assembled, all looking smart in their skimpy uniforms, their hair adorned with flowers and their spears shining. Lia felt very embarrassed to be naked when they all looked so fine, doubly so because of the clamps drawing attention to her nipples.

In the courtyard was an object that resembled a large stretcher, about six feet long and three wide, with handles at either end. It was covered by a red cloth, and towards the middle was a small stool, raised about ten inches above the surface. Lisbet pulled Lia across to the stool and motioned her to sit down. Lia lowered her backside gingerly onto the stool. Her ankles were grabbed and pulled back behind her, so that she was almost in a kneeling position, her knees and shins pressed against the cloth. A pair of shackles were attached to the base just beside her ankles, which were locked in place. Then the manacles on her wrists were secured to the stool behind her.

Once she was in position Shuna and Lisbet took hold of the chains attached to the nipple clamps. They pulled them tight, making Lia wince with pain. She tried to lean forward to ease the pressure, but was prevented by the cuffs at her wrists. The two Priestesses pulled the chains taut, then fastened them to the front of the platform. The clamps bit terribly as Lia's breasts were stretched forward.

At last Shuna and Lisbet were satisfied with their charge and four Priestesses gathered, one at each corner of the stretcher. On a command from Karla they lifted the poles onto their shoulders, then the order was given to open the gates.

Lia felt dreadfully exposed, and blushed as she thought of the sight she must make; her bare breasts stretched as they were, her legs pulled apart in a deliberate effort to make her sex visible to onlookers. And onlookers there were. Dozens of them, lining the street as she was carried along. This was the first time she had been permitted to leave the fortress since the New Moon Gathering, and the New Agers jostled for a sight of her.

The strange procession made its way through the streets, Karla leading, followed by Shuna and Lisbet, then Lia's litter, with the junior Priestesses bringing up the rear. All around were people, pointing and chattering. Lia stared straight ahead, unwilling to meet their eyes.

They were heading to the temple, and as they approached it another group of people appeared through its wide doorway. It was the High One, once again resplendent in his robes and being carried in his sedan chair. He too was surrounded by a large escort, and Lia's group joined behind his as they set off into the woods.

They weaved their way on through the pathways, Lia's litter swaying back and forth, so that the tension on her nipples became almost unbearable at times. They seemed to travel a long way, the marchers chanting as they went, the hot sun beating down on them. The path twisted this way and that, and the bearers were occasionally obliged to lower the litter to waist height to avoid Lia being hit by the lower branches of the trees. Glancing back, the procession stretched as far as she could see. It seemed as if the entire village had come out to see the ceremony.

Lia saw something she recognised. Standing by a pool of water was the unmistakable shape of the Tree of Birth, the strange plant beside which they had found her all those weeks before. Its branches were still adorned with fruit, the strange elongations on the trunk looking even more like stiff cocks in the bright sunlight.

In front of the tree was a large table, set out like an altar and draped with coloured cloths. They placed the High One's chair down before it, with Lia's litter alongside. The High One rose and went to the altar. He bowed low before it, then turned to the crowd and shouted something that Lia could not understand. The crowd did though, for they chorused a reply that was equally incomprehensible.

As always the call and response session went on for some time. It seemed to be an essential part of all their rituals. Occasional phrases were just understandable, but most of what was said was just gabble to Lia. She closed her eyes, trying to forget the throbbing pain in her nipples, and the heat in her groin that the pain was engendering.

At last the first phase of the ceremony came to an end. The silence caught Lia by surprise. She had been almost dozing, the strange rhythm of the mantras dulling her senses. She looked up, just in time to see the High One make a sign to the Priestesses. They gathered around her, and she felt the shackles being removed from her wrists and ankles. They took the clips from her nipples. They had become almost numb, but now they pulsed anew as the blood coursed through them once more. Lia longed to rub them, but feared what the Priestesses might do to her if she did.

Shuna and Lisbet helped her to her feet. Her legs were stiff from the confinement and at first she was unsteady, but she managed to stay erect. The two Priestesses led her to the altar.

"Stand on it," Shuna quietly ordered.

Lia turned her back and levered herself into a sitting position on the table, then climbed to her feet. Without waiting to be told she spread her legs and placed her hands behind her head. The Priestesses gathered round the altar, standing shoulder to shoulder on all four sides. Lia glanced at them, wondering what would happen next. She was extremely tense, listening for the explosions that would herald her release. But then Karla barked an order and Lia realised with a shock that the Priestesses had raised their spears, aiming them at her. She stood perfectly still, not daring to move an inch as she felt the sharp tips of the spears touch her body, a low chant rising from the Priestesses. For a terrible second Lia thought she was about to be killed like some barbaric sacrifice on a pagan altar. Then came another order from Karla and they lowered their spears and stood back from the altar.

What was to happen next Lia never found out, for at that moment an explosion boomed from the woods just beyond the altar. For a second she forgot Delgado's instructions and looked across to where a great column of dust rose up above the trees. Almost simultaneously a second blast occurred, even louder than the first, and Lia remembered her instructions. She surveyed the crowd. All eyes were in the direction of the explosions, and some people were running towards them.

Lia looked out to the west. At first she saw nothing, just a dense screen of trees. Then she spotted a movement, and as she watched her rescuers broke clear of the undergrowth. There were three of them, riding hard toward her. In the front she could make out Delgado, the other two strangers to her. They were galloping fast and Lia felt sure the New Agers would hear their approach, but a third explosion rocked the woods, its echoes drowning the sound of the approaching hoof beats.

Lia took her chance. In a single graceful movement she leapt down from the altar and began running out to intercept the horsemen. She saw Karla glance in her direction. It took the Priestess a matter of seconds to understand what was happening, but seconds were all Lia needed. Already she was clear of the crowd and heading towards her rescuers.

Behind her she heard shouts and glanced over her shoulder to see Shuna and Lisbet running after her. Delgado was very close, his arm outstretched, and she ran for all she was worth. As Delgado reached down to grab her Lia saw Shula unleash her spear. But it was too late. The weapon clattered harmlessly to the ground as she was hoisted onto Delgado's horse.

He dragged her up and she lay face down across his mount in front of him. Then with one hand on her back to steady her he was off, galloping back into the trees, leaving the New Agers to watch helplessly as he bore Lia away.

Chapter 16

Lia hung helplessly across the saddle as the horses galloped on, twisting and turning down the narrow woodland paths. It was all she could do to maintain her balance. She had never been on a horse before and the roughness of the ride took the wind out of her. All she could see was a blur of green as the ground rushed by. The pounding of the horse's hooves rang in her head, but she didn't mind the discomfort. The important thing was that she was getting away, every second putting more and more distance between her and the New Agers, closer and closer to Thorkil.

They rode on for more than an hour, heading ever further into the forest, and when at last they did come to a halt it was an exhausted Lia that was lowered to the ground.

The three men dismounted and gathered around her. For the first time she was able to take a good look at Delgado's companions. The first of them was small and swarthy. He had a thin, drawn face and a black droopy moustache that seemed to give him a permanent scowl. His eyes were narrow and sly and he looked her up and down with a knowing leer. Delgado introduced him as Mex.

The second man was called Chet. In contrast to Mex he was tall and broad-shouldered, with short brown hair and a broken nose. Lia guessed he had been a boxer in his time. He too stared at the naked girl with undisguised interest.

"Shit, Delgado," he said, "you didn't tell us she was gorgeous."

"Yeah," put in Mex, "and where's her fucking clothes?"

"She hasn't got any," replied Delgado with a laugh. "You're always flashing that bare cunt of yours, aren't you darling? Even keeps it shaved to give us a better look."

Lia said nothing, her eyes cast down.

"Come on girlie," said Delgado. "Let's see you standing properly. You may not be with those nutters any more, but we still expect you to know your place."

Slowly, reluctantly, Lia took up her submissive stance, her hands behind her neck and her legs apart. She was beginning to feel a little uneasy with her rescuers. This was not quite what she had expected.

Mex and Chet both grinned as they saw how subservient she was, their eyes roving over her bare breasts.

"That's better," said Delgado. "The boys and I expect a little respect from you. Understand?"

"Yes Sir," she replied quietly.

"Jeez those tits are gorgeous," said Mex.

"Go ahead and have a feel," said Delgado. "She won't stop you."

Mex reached out and took Lia's breasts in his hands. He squeezed, his fingers caressing the hardening nipples. Lia stared ahead, not wishing to catch his eye.

"We gonna have a little fun with her before you give her to Helda?" asked Chet.

"Helda?" Lia pulled away from Mex and turned to stare at Delgado.

"Wassamatter," he said. "Something bothering you?"

"He said you were going to hand me over to Helda!"

"So what?"

"You're supposed to be taking me to Thorkil! You promised!"

"Thorkil, Helda, what difference does it make? You'll be back with the Bikers whichever way."

"But you can't turn me over to Helda. She's a dreadful woman. It was her I was running away from in the first place!"

"Do you think I don't know that?" said Delgado. "Take a look at this." He turned to his saddlebag and pulled out a magazine. Lia recognised it as the Black Cat's prospectus.

"Where did you get that?" she gasped.

"I've had it for a long time," he replied. "I recognised you the first time I saw you."

"Show me," said Mex.

Delgado opened it to the page featuring Lia's naked body and read some of the text out to them.

"Wow," said Mex. "You sound like quite a girl."

"Listen," said Lia pleadingly, "you mustn't send me back there. If you return me to Thorkil I'm sure he'd pay you well."

"After I've been fucking his girl at every opportunity during the last couple of weeks? I doubt it somehow."

Lia blushed. "You wouldn't have to tell him," she said.

"Yeah, but you might."

"I wouldn't. I promise. Please take me back to Thorkil."

"Nope," said Delgado. "It's got to be Helda. I owe her a favour, and you're it. Meanwhile Mex and Chet here are looking forward to having a bit of fun."

"Yeah," said Mex, still groping her breasts. "Let's get it together, baby."

Lia was stunned as the extent of Delgado's trickery sank in. All this time she had given herself to him in the belief she was to be returned to Thorkil. Now those hopes were dashed, and she was actually going back into Helda's clutches. She stared at the three faces; Delgado grinning, Chet eyeing her and licking his lips, and Mex's hands all over her.

Suddenly something in Lia's brain seemed to snap. With a heave she brought her knee up into Mex's groin, catching him squarely in the balls. He doubled over in pain, groaning loudly. Before anyone had a chance to react she swung round and disposed of Chet in the same way, this time kicking out with her foot and striking him in his most sensitive area.

Delgado made a lunge for her but she was too quick for him, sidestepping at the last second and tripping him so he fell heavily, striking his head on a rock. All three were sprawled on the ground, two of them clutching their groins and moaning in unison while the third lay still, blood running from his forehead.

Lia knew she didn't have much time. She ran to the horses but realised she had no idea even how to mount, let alone ride one. So instead she slapped them on their rear quarters, making them kick their hind legs in the air and gallop away in panic. Having disposed temporarily of the three men's transport she was off, plunging into the woods without a backwards glance. She ran with all the speed she was able, turning down one path after another in an effort to confuse them. Her heart was pounding in her chest but she dare not slow down for a moment, leaping over fallen trees and stumps in her desperate effort to put as much distance between herself and the men as she could.

At last it all became too much and she slowed her pace, first to a trot, then to a walk. She tried her best to calm her nerves. After all, even if they were following her they were a long way behind. It seemed impossible that they could have traced the zigzag path she had taken through the trees. No, she was certain that she was well away from them now. She walked on, trying to keep going in the same direction, in the hope that she might soon find some kind of landmark. She came upon a pool and gratefully bent down to drink, splashing some of the water onto her face and breasts to cool herself. Nearby was a bush covered with berries, and she tasted one. It was sweet and juicy, and she picked a handful and sat down beside the pool to eat them.

Evening was coming on and she felt strangely relaxed in this peaceful spot. For the first time in weeks she was free, although still lost and naked. Even so it felt good to be out of shackles. She lay down on the soft grass, intending only to rest for a moment, but before long she was in a deep sleep.

Chapter 17

Lia was woken by the rays of the early morning sun as they fell on her upturned face. For a few seconds she couldn't think where she was, and sat up, blinking wearily. Then it all came back to her. The rescue, the ride through the forest, her escape from her captors. And now she was lost and alone in the middle of this great forest. Some of her optimism of the day before had ebbed away overnight, and this morning she felt very lonely indeed.

She rose to her feet, stretching, making a lovely picture in the early light, her lithe young body arched so that her breasts were thrust invitingly forward. She sensed the erotic sight she made there in the clearing, and her hand strayed to her sex, feeling for her clitoris and exciting it briefly.

She bathed in the pool. The water was cold but she didn't care, her flesh covered in goose bumps as she splashed it over herself. She climbed out of the pool feeling considerably refreshed, brushing the droplets of moisture from her body. The warmth of the sun soon dried her, and she settled on the grass to eat some more berries and consider her position.

She had to keep moving, she knew that. But she also needed to know in which direction she should be travelling. In such a dense forest she could wander for days without finding a way out. She had been in this predicament before, and had climbed a tree to ascertain where to go, but this time the land was low and no tree stood up tall enough to make it a viable option. Her only hope would be to follow one of the game paths. After all, the animals ought to know which way they were going.

She found the path she wanted almost at once. It was wider and straighter than the others, and led directly away from the waterhole. She set off along it at a brisk pace. She kept her eye on the sun to make certain that she wasn't doubling back on herself. Progress seemed good, and she felt a new optimism as she went.

She had been walking for some time when she came across the wall. It was a brick wall, about twelve feet high, and it seemed to stretch for miles in both directions, cutting a swathe through the wood. On the top was barbed wire, designed to prevent it from being scaled. It was almost as if it surrounded a prison, or some other secure institution. The path ran alongside it, so the naked girl had no choice but to follow it, gazing up at the unfriendly edifice beside her.

For quite a distance the wall was unbroken, just monotonous red-brown bricks stretching endlessly on. Then Lia's eye was caught by a door. It was green, though the sun had long since faded it, and the paint was old and peeling. Lia stopped before it, wondering what could possibly be on the other side. She tried the handle, and was surprised to find it swung open when she pushed.

She hesitated, the handle still in her hand. The wall had clearly been built to exclude interlopers and she was reluctant to be taken as an intruder. On the other hand it held a promise of security, something behind which she might be able to hide and escape those she was convinced were still hunting her. Taking a deep breath she stepped through, allowing the door to slam shut behind her.

On the other side of the wall the landscape was somewhat different. There were still trees, but they were scattered more sparsely and the grass was shorter. The whole impression was of a park rather than wild forest, and the openness made Lia feel exposed and nervous. The further she walked the more vulnerable she felt, the less dense landscape making her feel more visible than before, and she found herself covering her breasts and sex with her hands and glancing nervously about. She walked a few yards more, then turned and stared back at the door. Perhaps this had been a bad idea.

All at once she found herself quickly retracing her steps. When she reached the door she snatched the handle, turning it quickly, but to her dismay it refused to open. She tugged at it hard, but it seemed to be locked and would not move an inch. After rattling it frantically a few more times she stopped trying and collapsed against the wood, gazing about forlornly. She had no choice now. She had to stay inside the wall.

There was a well-defined path leading away, and having no better plan she decided to follow it. The track led deeper into the park. Somehow leaving the wall increased her sense of insecurity. It had seemed like a sort of shelter as she'd followed it, and in her state anything that gave her the slightest cover was welcome. But here, in this park, there was very little in the way of shelter, and the more she walked the more open the scenery became.

She began to consider where she might be. It was clearly no natural place.

To produce a park like it and keep it cultivated would take a number of people, but who would bother to keep such an expanse of land so well? Then it struck her. She must be on the estate of one of the Aristos. It was an odd thing that there were still some landed gentry amid the chaos of the current landscape. Whilst the cities had degenerated into lawlessness and the highways had been taken over by the Bikers, most of the upper classes either fled or had their properties snatched by the likes of Helda, to be turned into service depots or pleasure houses such as the Black Cat. But a few had survived, generally by making pacts with the Bikers. Some of these people still exercised a good deal of authority over the locals and the Bikers had been shrewd enough to exploit this, striking deals whereby a percentage of their profits went to the lords of the manor. They in turn assisted in keeping the peace amongst those that lived in the nearby villages. In time they became known as the Aristos, and they tended to live secluded lives in their large houses.

And this, Lia was convinced, was an Aristo's park. Nobody else could possibly afford such a large acreage. The realisation made her more nervous still. The Aristos were rich and proud. What would they make of a waif like herself trespassing on their property? She had to get out of the estate as soon as she could. But how? Certainly not through the entrance she had come in by.

Suddenly Lia's imagination began to conjure up mental pictures of what might happen if she was caught. She saw herself dragged before the lord of the manor and prostrated before him. She imagined the sort of punishments that might be meted out on her for trespassing on private land. She saw herself strung up and whipped before the powerful owner.

But Lia's was no normal imagination, and as these images passed through her brain an odd feeling of arousal began to fill her. She gazed down at her jutting breasts, the nipples prominent, already hardened by her erotic thoughts. She took in her bare mound, an open invitation to anyone, and a powerful heat began to well up in her groin.

"Well, well, well."

Lia froze as she heard the voice behind her, then slowly she began to turn but the voice barked at her.

"No! Just stay exactly as you are."

It was a man's voice, and it held a note of authority that made Lia obey instinctively. She stayed still. Who had found her?

"What's going on?" a second voice said.

"Come and see what I've found."

"Blimey, who the hell is she?"

"Bloody trespasser."

"What's she doing here?"

"You may well ask."

Lia didn't move, her eyes closed in dread. She cursed herself for not ignoring the door in the wall. Now she was in trouble again. She wondered how they treated trespassers, and again her mind was filled with fearful images of punishment. She felt something hard press against her backside.

"Put your hands on your head and turn around."

Lia obeyed, her eyes cast down as she exposed her breasts and shaven sex to the men. There were indeed two of them, both dressed in khaki uniforms, both carrying a long truncheon. It was one of these she'd felt prodding her bum. Both men were tall and rough looking, their menacing appearance enhanced by their shaven heads. Their eyes were cold as they surveyed her.

"Why are you trespassing?" asked the first.

"I didn't mean to."

"How did you get in?"

"Through a door in the wall. It wasn't locked. But then when I tried to get out I couldn't open it."

"That'll be that damned east door," said the other one. "The electronic lock's been playing up for a couple of weeks now. I've been meaning to fix it."

"Well you'd better get it done before Her Ladyship finds out. You know how tough she is on security."

"Shit yeah. Do you reckon we'd better turn this bitch over to her?"

"Might not be a good idea; she's bound to find out how she got in and that'll put us in the shit."

"What the hell do we do with her then?"

"Let's just thrash the little slut then throw her out."

"We could have a bit of fun with her first."

"You mean fuck her?"

"Why not? After all, looks like she wants it."

Lia was listening to their conversation with alarm. Her greatest fear was that they hand her over to the authorities, so being simply thrown off the land was the best she could hope for. But then there was the thrashing, and what was to follow...

She barely had time to ponder that though, when the two men closed in on her. One of them took a pair of handcuffs from his pocket.

"Hands behind you," he ordered.

Lia obeyed at once, and felt the familiar coldness as her wrists were clamped together. A second pair of cuffs was then fitted just above her elbows, leaving her quite unable to move her arms. She was becoming familiar with bondage, and she was unable to suppress a slight thrill as she realised how vulnerable she was.

One of the men produced a length of rope, and secured it to her cuffs. Then the other end was thrown over one of the branches of the tree they were standing beneath, the man pulled the rope and she found her arms being dragged up, forcing her to bend forward. He continued to pull until she feared her shoulders might dislocate, then he secured it to a lower branch.

Lia was helpless, her naked body stooped forward so that her breasts dangled freely. Her head was down, making her hair drop over her face, obscuring it completely. She stared at the ground, trembling partly with fear, partly with anticipation of what was to come.

"Right young lady," said a voice at her ear. "It's time you learnt your lesson. Trespassing is a pretty serious offence round here, and I'm going to leave a few marks on that pretty little backside of yours to remind you of that. And to remind you not to wander about bare-arsed in public. Do you understand?"

"Yes Sir," whispered Lia.

Thwack!

She lurched forward as the blow hit her square on the rear. It had come more suddenly than she expected and she gave a little yelp as her flesh burned. She craned her head round to see that the man had removed the thick leather belt at his waist, and was using it to punish her.

Thwack!

Once again the belt came down on her perfectly offered bottom, making a wide red mark across her flesh.

Thwack!

"What is going on here?"

The voice was a woman's, though Lia could not see her face from the position she was in. The beating stopped immediately and she heard the two men's boots snap together. Clearly the new arrival was someone important.

"I asked what you're doing. Who's she?"

"Trespasser, Your Ladyship."

"What have you done with her clothes?"

"She was like this when we found her, Ma'am."

Lia felt a hand take hold of her hair and snatch her head round so she was looking up at the new arrival. It was a young woman, about twenty-five years old. She wore a cotton shirt, beneath which were outlined large and shapely breasts. She also had on a pair of faded blue jeans that hugged her slim figure. She had a mane of long blonde hair that hung down her back in tresses. She stared intently at Lia with bright blue eyes.

"How did you get in?"

"I... I came through the door."

The woman turned on the guards. "Which door?"

"The east door, Your Ladyship. The lock's faulty."

"Then why hasn't it been repaired?"

"I'll see to it, Ma'am."

"Make sure you do. Anyone could have come trespassing. Just consider yourselves lucky it was only some local village tart on the lookout for business."

Lia wanted to object to such a slur, but felt it prudent to remain silent. She was still feeling very uncomfortable, suspended as she was, and her backside was stinging from the belt.

"Right," said the woman dismissively, "continue with the thrashing then chuck her out, though I suspect you'll want to screw her first. I'm going to the house now to prepare for this evening's..."

She broke off and turned back to Lia.

"Wait a minute though," she murmured thoughtfully.

With a shock Lia felt the woman's hand cup her breast, feeling its firmness. Then her other hand slipped through Lia's legs from behind, and she gave a sharp intake of breath as she felt herself probed.

"She's certainly sensitive," said the woman. "How many strokes did you give her?"

"Just three, Ma'am."

"Three, eh? It seems to have turned her on. Just look at the way she's responding to my finger."

She twisted her hand and was rewarded by a gasp from the tethered girl.

"I think I've changed my mind," said the woman suddenly. "Bring her to the house. She'll be an invaluable addition to tonight's little party. Hand her over to the housekeeper and tell her to get her cleaned up, then deliver her to my room, just as she is. Get on with it now."

And with that she turned and strode away.

Chapter 18

The two men marched Lia in the direction the woman had gone, holding the rope that was still attached to her manacles and shoving her forward in front of them. Lia progressed with her head down, trying to ignore the lewd remarks the men made as they eyed her lovely rear. The pair were obviously disgruntled at having missed their fun and grumbled on about the Countess, the young woman who had stopped her punishment.

The park seemed vast and it was some time before the house came in sight. It was very large with turrets and mock battlements. It was surrounded by a wide green lawn across which the men took her, the grass soft under her feet after the stony path they'd been following. They led her to a rear entrance, the door large and imposing with a short flight of stone steps leading up to it. Lia was made to halt on the top step while one of the men tugged on a brass bell-pull.

The woman who came to the door looked none too friendly. She was in her fifties, short and overweight with a menacing gleam in her eye. When she saw Lia her jaw dropped. "Who on earth is this?" she asked in astonishment.

"Just a trespasser," said one of the men.

"What, walking about like that? She should be ashamed of herself. Why have you brought her here? She's no concern of mine."

"The Countess said to."

"Her Ladyship?"

"That's right. Said you were to give her a bath, then take her to Her

Ladyship's room, just as she is."

"What, with no clothes on?"

"That's what she said."

The woman shook her head. "I don't know," she grumbled. "The goings on in this house. It never would have happened in her grandfather's day. At least he was discreet."

"Look," said the man, "are you going to take her or not? Only we've got work to do."

"I suppose if Her Ladyship said so I'll have to. Where are the keys to the handcuffs?"

"Here," said the man, handing them over. "But be careful. It's my guess she'll try to escape."

"Not from me she won't," said the woman sternly. She took the rope and dragged Lia through the door, slamming it shut in the faces of the two men. She led Lia down a short corridor to a kitchen where half a dozen maids were sitting at a table drinking tea. When they saw Lia they stared in astonishment, then burst into giggles.

"What on earth...?"

"Who's she?"

"What's going on?"

"Never you mind," barked the housekeeper. "Ellie, take her up to the bathroom. You'll have to manacle her to the pipes while she's washing. Apparently she's liable to try and run away."

"What, like that? She wouldn't dare. Why, the guards would..."

"That's enough," said the housekeeper firmly. "Just do as you're told. Flora, you'd better go too. And hurry up now."

Still giggling, two of the girls rose to their feet. They were both identically dressed in black maid uniforms with small white hats and white aprons. The one called Ellie took the rope from the housekeeper, spying the stripes across Lia's bum.

"Look," she said, pointing. "Someone's been thrashing her bottom."

"Best thing for her in the circumstances," said the housekeeper. "When she's had her bath I want you to bring her straight back to me. Understand?"

"Yes Miss Strong," chorused the girls as they dragged Lia out of the kitchen.

She was taken down a series of narrow hallways and up a flight of stairs into what she took to be the servants' quarters. They led her into an old fashioned bathroom, full of brass pipes and fittings with a bare wooden floor. They shut the door and slid a bolt across. Flora began filling the bath while Ellie saw to Lia's manacles, releasing her right wrist momentarily before clamping it round a sturdy pipe that ran beside the bath. Only then did she release her elbows.

Once the bath was full Lia was ordered into it. The water was hot and smelled of lavender, and she lay back. It felt wonderful to be relaxing at last

74

after her long ordeal since escaping the New Agers, and she stretched luxuriously, feeling her aches and pains melt away. She was not allowed to rest for long though. A bar of soap and a bottle of shampoo were handed to her, and the two maids stood back to watch as she began to wash.

As she was doing so she noticed the two youngsters whispering and giggling again. Flora nudged Ellie to her feet, and the girl went to a cabinet on the wall. She extracted something from it and handed it to Lia. It was a can of shaving foam and a razor. Her face burning, Lia raised herself until she was sitting on the edge of the bath. She spread the foam over her pubic mound and sex lips, and began gingerly shaving off the stubble that had grown there. The two maids sat watching, occasionally lapsing into fits of giggles.

At last Lia was done. She rinsed herself carefully, then placed the shaving implements on one side, looking up expectantly at her keepers. The two maids went through the process of manacling her again, first the elbows, then the wrists. Only then did they unbolt the door. They need not have been so cautious, for Lia had no incentive to escape just at the moment, especially with the two guards still patrolling the grounds.

They sat her on a stool and towelled her hair. Flora produced a hairdryer and began drying it, running a brush through Lia's flowing tresses as she did so. Unexpectedly Lia found herself rather enjoying their attentions, the brush having a soothing effect as it ran through her hair.

Once satisfied the job was complete they pulled her to her feet and led her out of the bathroom and back down to the kitchen. The housekeeper inspected her minutely, before at last pronouncing her presentable and fit to be taken to the Countess's room.

"Though how I can use the word presentable when she's completely nude I don't know," she complained. "Well, I suppose you'd better take her. Hurry now!"

At once Lia was on the move again, this time to a quite different part of the house. It was clearly where the owner lived. The halls were thickly carpeted and lined with oak panels. Large oil paintings hung from the walls, and the furnishings were antique. Lia padded along, her feet sinking into the plush floor coverings. The building seemed deserted apart from a few domestic servants, who stared at Lia as she passed, their jaws open. They reached a wide reception room, and she was guided up a sweeping staircase. At last they reached a door, where Ellie knocked timidly.

"Come."

Lia recognised the voice of the Countess.

The maid opened the door. "Please, Your Ladyship..." she began.

"Yes, all right Ellie. I see you have her with you. Leave the keys to her cuffs with me and be off with you."

"Yes Ma'am."

Ellie ushered Lia into the room, then placed the keys on a table and she and

Flora retreated, closing the door behind them. Lia stood glancing round uneasily. Like the rest of the house the room was sumptuously furnished, with a large four-poster bed at one end and a suite of comfortable chairs beside a window which overlooked the green lawns outside. The Countess was sitting in one of these chairs.

"Come over here," she instructed.

Obediently the tethered girl crossed the room and stopped in front of her.

"Do you always stand with your legs apart like that?"

Lia blushed. It was pure habit that made her stand as she did. She had been well trained by both the Bikers and the New Agers. She made to close her legs.

"No," said the woman sharply. "Stay as you are. I rather like you like that."

She rose to her feet and began to walk round Lia, who remained rooted to the spot.

"Such a pretty little thing you are," she murmured. "What gorgeous breasts. You're quite right to leave them bare. And that arse. Those red stripes across it look exquisite. Tell me, where are your clothes?"

"I haven't any, Your Ladyship."

"Why?"

"I lost them."

"When?"

"I can't remember. It was months ago."

"Months? Where have you been since then?"

"I was captured. By the Bikers. Then the New Agers got me."

"I think you'd better tell me the whole story."

So Lia recounted the full tale of her adventures, starting from the incident with the warden at her hostel, and going on to tell how she had run away, lost her clothes whilst swimming and been picked up by the Bikers. She told the story in full, leaving out no details under the woman's close questioning. She glowed red as she described the incident in the diner. She described the sale of her indenture at auction, and her life at the Black Cat. She went on to tell of her short-lived rescue, and her time with the New Agers. Finally she brought the story up to date, with her second rescue and subsequent escape. When she had finished the woman sat back and stared at her for a few minutes.

"Well, you have had an interesting time! And this Biker, the one you're in love with. What was his name again?"

"Thorkil, Your Ladyship. He's from Depot twenty-nine."

"Thorkil? Yes, I know of him."

Lia's eyes opened wide. "You do?"

"It's not so surprising. He's quite prominent among the Bikers. He's not local, though I know where to find him."

Lia stared in disbelief. For the first time since Helda's Bikers had attacked them in the forest there was news of Thorkil. Her heart beat fast, and then what she heard next made her want to shout with joy.

"I'll put in a call to his depot in the morning. See if he wants to come and get you."

"Thank you Mistress!" In her excitement and happiness she reverted to her old form of address.

"Mistress?"

"I'm sorry, Your Ladyship. It's what I used to call my superiors."

The woman smiled. "Don't worry, I rather like it. Perhaps we should find you some clothes before your Thorkil arrives."

Lia blushed. "Thorkil keeps me naked too," she mumbled.

"And I can see why," laughed the woman. "Now, young lady, I didn't ask you to stay here just to find your kinky Biker friend. I've got plans for you tonight."

"Your Ladyship?"

"I've got some friends coming for a little party this evening. Just some other girls. And you're going to help me entertain them. We need a man to liven things up."

"A man, Your Ladyship?"

The woman moved closer, so that Lia's breasts were almost brushing the fabric of her shirt.

"That's what I said."

"But..."

The woman held up a hand. "Listen, little Biker's girl," she said. "Around here I'm known as the Countess, but to you I'm your Mistress, and if you want to see your beloved Thorkil tomorrow you'll obey me utterly. All right?"

"Yes Mistress."

"Good. Behave yourself, and I think you're going to find it as much fun as I am."

The Countess rang a bell, and shortly afterwards Ellie and Flora presented themselves at the door.

"Come in here," she ordered, leading them into a small dressing room just off the main bedroom. The three disappeared and the sound of low voices drifted out, punctuated by drawers closing and occasional squeals of laughter. When the three emerged Flora was carrying a black bag, her face bright red.

"Take her away with you," ordered the woman. "And prepare her for tonight."

Once again Lia was led through the house by the two young maids, but this time they did not take her back to the kitchen. Instead they led her to a small room on the ground floor; some sort of study, with a leather-topped desk in it. They locked the door, then Flora set about undoing Lia's cuffs. It felt good to have her arms free again, and Lia stretched them up above her head.

Ellie dipped her hand into the mysterious bag and produced two leather wrist straps with rings attached. She ordered Lia to hold out her hands and secured them tightly onto each wrist. More straps were applied to her ankles, and a collar around her throat.

They sat her on a chair and Flora began to work on her hair once more, though this time the styling was to be quite different. She began pulling it back and plaiting it, then she curled it round on top of her head, pinning it there with hairclips. Then she produced a cap and put it on her, so that the plait was hidden beneath it. The whole affair was puzzling to Lia, and staring into a mirror on one wall she barely recognised her reflection.

"On your feet," ordered Ellie. "Over there. Sit on the desk and lie back."

Lia crossed to the desk and sat on it, the leather cold against her bottom. She leant back, lying with her legs dangling, then without waiting to be told she spread her thighs apart.

"Good," said the maid. She reached into the bag again and pulled something out. Lia stared at it in surprise. It was like nothing she had ever seen before. The object was a sort of double dildo. Two enormous rubber cocks, perfectly shaped and joined at the base so that they formed a V-shape. From the base of one of them dangled a pair of balls, looking extremely realistic. The two maids began giggling once more as they examined it.

"How does it work?" asked Flora.

"The two ends are connected," replied Ellie. "Look, when I squeeze the end of one the other one's end swells up."

Lia watched, her stomach full of butterflies, as Ellie demonstrated the thing to her friend.

"Just feel the shaft," went on Ellie. "It's got like a sheath on it that moves backwards and forwards, and when it does so the other one does the same."

"What's that little lever for at the base?" asked Flora.

"Whenever you move the sheath up and down or squeeze it the lever moves. It even does it when you squeeze the balls. Watch."

Ellie demonstrated, and Lia saw the little projection that curved back from the base of one of the dildos did indeed move back and forth in response to the manipulation of the other one. The whole thing was the most elaborate sex toy, and she felt a growing warmth between her thighs as she realised it was intended for her.

There were pink straps hanging from it, and Ellie spent a few seconds undoing them. "Hold her lips apart for me while I put it in," she said to Flora, and Lia felt a familiar thrill as she heard the words.

Lia could see Flora was unsure, and guessed the girl had never touched another pussy before. Her hands shook slightly as she placed them on Lia's leg. She ran them up Lia's thighs, pausing as she reached her crotch.

"Go on," said Ellie. "It won't bite."

Slowly Flora moved her hands higher, sliding her fingers to Lia's sex, stretching the lips apart. "Look, she's wet inside," she said to her companion, almost in awe. "She must be really turned on."

"Takes all kinds, I suppose," sniffed Ellie. "At least it'll make it easier to slip this thing into her."

It was all Lia could do to keep still as she felt the end of the dildo press against her exposed sex. At first the inexperienced girl had trouble penetrating her, despite Lia's own efforts to spread her thighs as wide as she was able.

"Give it a twist," suggested Flora.

Ellie tried again, turning the knob back and forth as she pressed, and at last it slipped into Lia's vagina, making her gasp as it stretched her love hole. Once she had been penetrated the wetness of her sex meant Ellie was able to feed the great cock into her more easily. She pushed, twisting it as she did so, sinking it deeper and deeper until it was completely buried within the girl and the moving lever was resting against her clitoris. Every time Ellie touched the dildo the lever would oscillate, rubbing against her sensitive bud and making her groan.

Ellie took the straps and fastened them. One was cinched tight round Lia's waist, with two more running diagonally over her bottom cheeks and between her legs to attach at the base of the balls. Two more ran down in a V in the front, fitting to small rings on either side of the dildo, leaving her bare pubis exposed. Ellie fussed with the straps, making them tight, then stood back.

"There," she said, "I think that'll do. Take a look at yourself in the mirror."

Lia found it slightly awkward to walk with the thick rubber cock filling her so completely. She stared at her reflection. What she saw was extraordinary.

It was as if she really did have a cock. A stiff, erect rod that rose from her groin like a flagpole, the balls dangling between her legs indistinguishable from the real thing. She stared at herself in astonishment. So this was what the Countess had meant about needing a man at the party. It explained the way they had made her hair look short, as well. The only thing they couldn't hide were her breasts, looking totally incongruous above the erect cock. She had been turned into a kind of hermaphrodite, and she felt a sudden thrill of lust as she realised what an erotic sight she made. Even the maids ceased their giggling as they took her in, starring wide-eyed. Nothing was said as they circled the naked girl, taking in every inch of her.

The sound of the door handle turning brought them back to their senses, and they swung round guiltily as the mistress of the house entered.

"Oh yes," she said, ignoring the maids, her eyes fastened on Lia. "That's perfect. You look absolutely gorgeous."

Lia glowed red, and did not reply.

"Come here," ordered the Countess, and Lia crossed to where she stood. She stopped in front of her, her face reddening even more as she contemplated the obscene cock that separated them.

The Countess reached down and gave the bulbous tip of the dildo a squeeze, causing the end deep in Lia's vagina to swell and the lever to rub her clitoris. Lia gasped at the sensation, her sex giving an involuntary spasm that caused the tip in the Countess's hand to swell. The reaction was not lost on the woman, who smiled.

"I see it's giving you some pleasure too," she said. Lia dropped her eyes.

"Right." The woman turned to her maids. "Take her to the party room and get her ready. My guests will be here soon."

Chapter 19

The voices of the Countess's guests increased Lia's nerves as she waited for the party to begin. They were so close, yet she was unable to see them. She tugged at her bonds but they held her fast. She had no choice but to wait to be introduced to the guests, standing against the wall, her wrists chained to rings on either side of her, stretching her arms wide and high above her head. Her ankles too were trapped, secured to more chains attached to the floor, so that her body was held in a great X. She made an extraordinary sight, the stiff pink penis jutting from her groin like a permanent erection.

The maids had secured her behind a curtain that hid her from the rest of the room. She had heard the Countess's guests arriving, and now they chatted and laughed on the other side of the curtain, their conversation punctuated by the occasional pop of a champagne cork. She waited with apprehension for the curtain to slide aside, for her to be exposed in all her naked glory, erect penis and all.

Eventually she heard the words she had been anticipating with a mixture of dread and suppressed excitement.

"Amy, what's behind the curtain?"

Lia froze, her heart beating fast, wondering if the others would take up the theme. They did.

"Yes," came another voice, "it wasn't there last time we came. What is it Amy?"

"It's a little secret," replied the Countess.

"A secret! I love secrets. What is it, some new stud you've found to fuck us?"

"It's better than that. This stud isn't going to lose his erection after a few screws."

"What do you mean?"

"Oh go on, Amy, show us!"

Lia's trepidation grew as she listened. The women were curious, and she knew that in a few moments she would be exposed to them. She looked down at herself, at her firm breasts, the nipples made hard by the thrill of bondage, at the dildo that filled her vagina, that forced her legs apart even without the chains that held her spread wide. She felt a deep sense of shame, but at the same time enormously aroused, and the cock twitched as her vagina contracted around it.

The room was quiet now and the clip of the Countess's shoes echoed as she made her way to where Lia was hanging. The curtain rustled, and Lia knew her mistress was holding it. There was a long pause, she held her breath, then with a flourish the curtain was pulled aside.

"Wow!"

"My God, Amy, that's incredible!"

"Who is she? It is a she, isn't it?"

"Look at that cock!"

Lia stared at the four women, blushing furiously as she was exposed to them. They were all in their mid-twenties, beautiful to look at and expensively dressed. What must they think of her, naked and chained and filled by the grotesque sex toy?

The guests gathered round her, chatting excitedly as the Countess explained where Lia had come from.

"A Biker's girl?" said one. "Lucky Biker."

"Just look at those gorgeous tits," said another. "And the way you've tied her; it's so sexy."

"But what a cock! Can I touch it?"

"Of course you can," their hostess replied. "For tonight her orders are to do whatever you wish. And she's very obedient, as I think you'll find."

One of the women reached for Lia's breasts, running her hands over them and feeling the hardness of her nipples, fully erect and protruding invitingly.

Another reached for her cock. "Ahh..." Lia sighed as the woman squeezed the bulbous tip and the clitoris stimulator rubbed against her love bud.

The woman turned to her hostess, her eyes wide. "She's acting as if it's really her cock."

"That's right. Every time you touch it she gets stimulated. And she's a randy little thing. I've never seen a girl so easily turned on. She used to work at the Black Cat, you know."

"Not the one called Lia?" asked one of the guests. "Always kept naked?"

"Yes, this is her," replied the Countess, looking pleased with herself. "And tonight she's ours."

"Oh how wonderful! I was told she took on a whole roomful of chaps one night, and was ready for more in the morning."

"I heard that too."

Lia stared at the women, astonished that they could know her name. It was obvious that the fame of the Black Cat spread wider than she had imagined.

"Oh, Amy, I've just got to have her. Where's the key to these chains?" The woman who spoke was blonde, with sparkling green eyes. She wore a tight mini-dress that hugged her figure like a second skin. She was braless, and her nipples were clearly outlined against the clinging material. Lia felt a spasm of excitement as she heard the words, and looked expectantly at her mistress.

"Have her now if you like, Barbara."

The Countess handed the woman some keys, and as she undid the bonds Lia could tell the woman was intensely aroused, barely able to insert them in the locks such was the trembling of her hands. But at last Lia was free and

Barbara dragged her out to the middle of the floor.

"Put on some music," she shouted. "I want to dance with my new young man."

Somebody touched a button and the room was filled with a throbbing beat. Barbara began to dance, her body shaking to the rhythm of the music. For a few seconds Lia watched in fascination, unable to take her eyes off her lithe body.

"Dance, girl," ordered the Countess, above the music. "You're here to entertain my guests, remember."

Obediently Lia too began to move, placing her hands behind her head and gyrating her hips so that the phallus that projected from her groin rotated provocatively. Her dance was totally instinctive, like some primitive tribal ritual. She closed her eyes, allowing the beat to carry her as she swung her hips back and forth. The other guests looked on with fascination, watching the muscles in her backside contract as she thrust her pelvis at her partner.

Suddenly Barbara's emotions seemed to overcome her. She moved closer, pulling Lia to her. Lia melted into the arms of her partner like a lover, their breasts together, the pink cock trapped between them.

Barbara placed her lips over Lia's and Lia opened her mouth eagerly, allowing the woman's tongue to enter. She held her close, grinding her hips, making small mewing sounds as her sex was stimulated by the dildo.

"It really turns you on when I touch your cock, doesn't it?" the woman purred.

"Yes Ma'am."

"Is that right, Amy?" Barbara asked.

"I told you. It's designed to give her as much pleasure as a real cock would," replied the Countess.

Barbara reached down and began playing with the balls that dangled between the girl's legs. Each squeeze brought a wave of pleasure to Lia as the lever rubbed against her hard little love bud.

"And she's certainly turning me on," gasped Barbara. "I've got to have her on my own."

"Go ahead," said the Countess. "She's all yours."

Barbara grabbed Lia's hand. "Come on," she said, "it's time to give Barbara what she wants." She dragged Lia off into a room next door, the study where Lia had been prepared for the party. As soon as the door was closed she moved in on Lia.

"Unzip me quick," she ordered. "I've just got to have my tits sucked. Come on, get a move on."

Lia slipped down the zip that held the woman's dress closed. The garment dropped to the floor, to be kicked aside by its owner. Lia stared. Barbara's breasts were large and shapely with big brown aureoles surrounding her nipples. All she wore now was a pair of black briefs and a matching black suspender belt and stockings.

"Suck my tits," she ordered quietly.

Lia leant forward and placed her lips to Barbara's nipples. She began to suck, and as she did the nipple swelled to hardness in her mouth, thick and rubbery. Lia slurped greedily, toying with the woman's other nipple with her fingers. Barbara's breathing became heavy as the girl stimulated her, and she pressed her chest forward against Lia's face.

"That's it," she whispered. "Suck me you gorgeous, randy little bitch." Lia responded, eliciting a groan from Barbara, whose hand reached down for the dildo. She squeezed its tip, making Lia squirm with the exquisite sensation of it.

Lia transferred her lips to Barbara's other breast, nibbling the protruding tip while her tongue worked back and forth over it. The taste of the woman's flesh was extraordinary and she found herself tingling with the prospect of what was to come.

"My knickers," murmured Barbara. "Pull them off. Do it now."

Lia dropped to her knees. She grasped the waistband of Barbara's panties and dragged them all the way down in a single movement, lifting the woman's feet and pulling the flimsy garment off. She stared at her companion's crotch, covered in short dark hairs trimmed to a perfect triangle. Her sex lips were pink and thick. Hesitantly Lia reached for them, prising them gently apart and feeling for Barbara's clit, bringing a low moan from her as she felt the hard little nodule.

"Oh fuck..." moaned Barbara. "Lick me, for goodness sake."

Lia moved her face closer, her nostrils filling with the woman's arousal. She protruded her tongue, sliding it between the pink lips, and Barbara gave a sharp intake of breath as Lia found that sensitive spot only just vacated by her fingers. She slid her tongue inside, darting it back and forth. Barbara grabbed Lia's hair, pressing her face against her sex as she writhed in ecstasy.

"Over to the desk," she whispered. "Come on."

Barbara placed her backside on the edge, then lay back, her open sex framed between her black suspenders. She grabbed the end of Lia's cock, making her gasp with pleasure once more. "Stick it in me," she ordered. "I want to be fucked properly while I watch those delicious tits of yours."

The tip of the phallus glistened with moisture as Lia brushed it over the woman's sex lips, teasing Barbara's clitoris.

"Fuck me little boy-girl," Barbara said through gritted teeth. "Stick that fucking cock in me and give me a good screwing."

This time there was no hesitation on Lia's part. She positioned the cock at the mouth of Barbara's vagina and shoved her hips forward. The two cried out in chorus as the length slipped into Barbara's sex. Every sensation felt by Barbara was transmitted with equal intensity to Lia, who revelled in the joy it gave her. She buried the cock deep, so that the balls were brushing her companion's bottom. She began to fuck the woman, her hips pumping back and forth as the glorious sensations filled her too, the secret lever bringing her to new heights with every stroke.

All the time she was being fucked Barbara kept her eyes on Lia, watching her lovely breasts bounce with the rhythm of her thrusts. Lia's mouth was open, gasping for breath, a trickle of sweat running down between her breasts as she rammed the dildo home. Lia glanced across at the mirror on the wall. The sight was extraordinary, the two women naked apart from Barbara's suspenders and stockings, joined together by their cunts, the shaft of the dildo gleaming with wetness as it ploughed in and out.

Suddenly Barbara lifted her backside clear of the desk, thrusting up at Lia, and she knew the woman's climax was upon her. She redoubled her efforts, her hips pumping back and forth as she felt her own peak approaching.

The two came together, both screaming, oblivious that they could be heard in the next room as they drowned in the pleasure of the moment, the dildo making a sucking sound with the copious juices that flowed from both of them.

When they were finally spent Lia slid the cock out of her companion, who was stretched out across the desk, her eyes closed, a blissful smile on her face. "Mmm," she murmured, "that was lovely."

"Hey Barbara," shouted a voice from the next room. "Don't hog her. Let's have her back out here. We need her too."

Barbara waved a weary hand at Lia. "You heard them," she said. "Get back in there."

Lia left her where she was and re-entered the party room. What she saw there made her stop short. Where she had been shackled to the wall, one of the other women had taken her place. She was dark and petite, with hazel brown eyes and pouting lips. Quite how they had done it was not clear, as she was evidently not happy, struggling with her bonds and cursing her friends. The Countess was approaching her with a pair of scissors.

"Don't you dare, Amy," warned the trapped woman. "This dress cost me a fortune."

"You can afford it, Mandy," laughed her hostess. Mandy was wearing a long slinky gown that was slit all the way up to her hip on one side. A thin strap ran round her throat and the low neckline revealed the cleavage between a pair of small but beautifully formed breasts.

Mandy gave a shriek as the Countess slid the scissors into the top of the dress's slit and began to cut. Mandy was struggling for all she was worth, but there was no hope. The manacles held her fast. All she could do was watch in dismay as the scissors snipped their way up the dress until they reached her armpit. The dress fell open, revealing brief panties and bra underneath. A final snip at the neckband and the dress was just a pile of useless material on the floor. Mandy stared down at it in dismay, then up at her enigmatic hostess.

"You bitch," she hissed. "That was brand new."

"Bitch, am I?" said the Countess, amused. "I'm afraid that remark just lost you your underwear too."

"No!" shouted Mandy. "Leave me!"

But it was already too late. With three quick snips her bra was rendered useless, falling to the floor beside the dress. Mandy's naked breasts were a sight to behold, firm and round like ripe oranges, the nipples small and hard. Mandy gave another squeal as the Countess set about her briefs, and in no time she was naked, pinned to the wall like some biological specimen, her friends surrounding her.

"You rotten cows!" shouted Mandy, but somehow her anger made her even more lovely, standing with her legs forced apart, so that her black pubic curls and the pinkness of her sex were revealed for all to see. Lia licked her lips; she could see why others found her irresistible when chained, and the thought of it sent a spasm through her that made the penis twitch visibly.

"Look," said one of the other women, "our little boy-girl is turned on by the sight of Mandy's cunt."

"Then she shall have what she desires," said their hostess, a smile spreading across her face. "Young lady, I want to watch you fucking Mandy."

"No!" snarled Mandy. "You mustn't. Not in front of everybody." But she was helpless to resist as Lia was led forward.

The Countess took hold of the phallus and guided the helmet towards Mandy's open sex, ignoring her protests.

"No Amy. You mustn't. You mustn't... oh!"

The tone of her voice changed as Lia pushed the dildo deep into her, their erect nipples brushing together in a way Lia found deliciously stimulating. She began to move her hips back and forth, quickly finding a rhythm. The session with Barbara had already taught her something of taking the man's role, and her hips moved smoothly back and forth as she screwed the protesting woman; protests already becoming more and more feeble as the sex began to have its desired effect. Mandy was moaning now, and beginning to match Lia's thrusts with her own.

"Kiss me, you disgusting little minx," she said quietly. "Kiss me like you kiss that Biker of yours. Kiss me like you really mean it."

Lia responded at once, wrapping an arm around Mandy and pulling her closer, their breasts squashed together. She forced her tongue into Mandy's mouth, increasing the strength of her thrusts as she did so, making Mandy's bare backside slap against the wall behind her. Lia glanced at the other women out of the corner of her eye. The Countess and her two companions were watching intently, the smiles on their faces replaced by dreamy arousal. A moan made them glance towards the door, where Barbara was leaning against the frame, her legs spread wide. She was still wearing only stockings and suspenders, her fingers in her vagina, masturbating vigorously.

Mandy's orgasm was loud and long, her cries matched by those of Lia and Barbara as the three women climaxed together. Lia held Mandy close, continuing to ram the dildo deep inside her until she felt the captive relax in her chains. Then she withdrew, leaving the woman hanging spread-eagled where she was, and turned to the others.

"Right, who's next?" asked the Countess.

Chapter 20

Lia rolled onto her back and opened her eyes. For a second she couldn't think where she was. Then she remembered the Countess. She looked about sleepily. She was lying on a sun lounger beside a swimming pool. All about were empty bottles and glasses, and lying on the terrace beyond she could see the discarded double dildo. She was alone. The rest of the revellers seemed to have gone inside, leaving her where she slept.

She had no idea what time the party ended, but by the finish she was utterly exhausted. She had been made to fuck all five women, a task she had carried out gladly, sharing their orgasms on every occasion. Then they had come out to the pool terrace, where the antics continued, the women all stripping naked and diving into the water before returning to Lia to be fucked again in any possible position. Lia soon lost count of the number of orgasms she'd had as she continued her male role, pandering to the whims of her lustful mistress and her companions.

At last, when she could go no further, they let her rest, unstrapping the phallus from her and sliding it into themselves. Lia fell asleep to the groans and sighs of the women as they pleasured themselves.

She gazed dozily up at the starry sky, thinking of the following day, when she would finally get her Thorkil back. With a sigh of contentment she rolled over and fell asleep.

"Wake up."

Something hard was prodding Lia in the ribs and she shifted uncomfortably.

Whack! This time it was a stroke across the backside which stung her into wakefulness.

"Wake up I said."

Lia gazed up into the morning sunlight, still not fully comprehending what was happening.

"Tie her and gag her. We don't want her alerting anybody."

Lia hands were seized and trapped behind her at the wrists and elbows. Then something was forced between her teeth; a rubber ball that filled her mouth so she was unable to speak. A pair of straps went round her head and fastened at the back, holding it in place.

Rough hands grabbed her and hauled her to her feet. She stood uncertainly in the early light, trying to focus her eyes. Then she recognised her captors. It was the two security guards.

The taller of the two eyed her up and down. Having her arms trapped as they were caused her breasts to thrust forward, and he took them in his hands, his coarse fingers mauling her soft white skin. For the first time she noticed he had three stripes on his arm, and the other had only two.

"Right," he said, "you're coming with us."

Lia tried to protest, but with the gag in her mouth it was impossible. She wanted to run away, but already one of the guards had attached a lead to her chains and was pushing her forward.

"March," he said. "And get a move on or you'll feel my truncheon on your arse again."

Lia had no choice. She set off across the lawn with the men close behind her. She couldn't understand what was happening. She had been convinced of the Countess's sincerity in promising to reunite her with Thorkil, so where were they taking her?

"Get a move on," said the man with the three stripes. "And don't make a sound."

Perhaps the men were acting against the Countess's will, and they had some other purpose in mind for her. She thought of the whipping they had begun on the previous day, and her apprehension deepened. She gave a despairing glance over her shoulder at the house, but all was quiet, and while the Countess slept, she was being carried off once more.

They made an odd sight as they marched on through the park, the two men in their quasi-military uniforms, preceded by the naked girl, still wearing the collar fitted for the party, her breasts thrust forward, hard nipples indicating that the bondage was arousing her.

"You sure we'll get away with this, Sarge?" It was the first time either of them had spoken since they left the house, and her heart sank as she heard her fears confirmed. They were definitely not obeying the orders of the Countess.

"Don't worry," came the reply, "we simply say she escaped. After all, they left her out on that terrace all night. What did they expect? She just found her way back to the east door. Her Ladyship knows now the lock's faulty."

"I guess so."

"Well let's face it, she's just some slut as far as they're concerned. They'll have forgotten about her in a couple of days."

Ahead of them Lia could see the wall looming, and the small door through which she had entered the day before. She wondered why she was being taken there. At first she thought maybe the two men wanted to fuck her, to take the pleasure they were denied the day before, but there seemed to be more than that. What could they possibly want?

They reached the door and the sergeant opened it. He pushed her through onto the dusty path outside.

"Well, well, well. Look who's here."

Lia gave a gasp into her gag. There were three men standing there - Delgado, Mex and Chet.

Delgado moved forward, taking the lead from the sergeant and dragging her close to him. "I bet you weren't expecting to see us again, you crafty little bitch," he growled. Lia wouldn't have been able to find an answer even if her mouth hadn't been filled by the gag.

Delgado turned to the guards. "You've done well," he said. "She give you any trouble?"

"Came quiet as a lamb," the sergeant replied.

"Good. I'll see to it you get rewarded for this. Probably end up with a security job at the Black Cat. Good money and a few perks, like this little one."

"You're gonna hand her over to Helda then?"

"Sure, just as soon as we can."

"We've got a little score to settle first, though, haven't we?" sniggered Chet.

"We certainly have." Delgado grabbed Lia's hair, pulling her face up to his. "That little escape plot of yours caused me and my pals a good deal of pain."

"As well as the trouble of finding you again," put in Mex.

"You gonna thrash her?" asked the sergeant.

"Too bloody right we are," said Chet. "Wanna watch?"

The sergeant grinned. "Certainly do," he said.

Lia glanced fearfully from one to another. From the moment she realised she was back in the hands of Delgado and his friends she knew she would be punished. After the way she had escaped it was inevitable. She would have preferred it to happen without the guards watching, but Delgado held all the cards. So when they ordered her to stand under a branch of a nearby tree she did as she was told. It was most unlikely they would give her another chance to escape.

The sergeant released her arms and her wrists were seized by Mex and Chet, who bound each one with rope, tied tightly. Then they made her raise her arms up to the overhanging branch. At full stretch she could just touch the branch, and they tied her hands there a shoulder's width apart, hauling her almost onto tiptoes to do it, leaving her body taut, her breasts stretched slightly. Once they were sure she was secure Delgado removed her gag, tossing it to the sergeant.

Lia felt very vulnerable trussed there in front of the three men, naked and helpless. Delgado took full advantage, stroking her firm breasts. He slid his hand down and slipped a finger into her sex, twisting his hand as he did so. Lia closed her eyes, trying to suppress the emotions his touch aroused in her.

The sound of cracking wood made her look over Delgado's shoulder. Behind him Mex had cut a cane from the undergrowth. It was thin and whippy and he was swishing it through the air. She knew he would soon be using it on her bare backside, and the thought sent a shameful thrill through her that caused the muscles of her sex to contract. Delgado felt it, and his grin broadened.

"I think she's looking forward to this," he said. "Her cunt's fairly throbbing."

"Let me feel," said the sergeant. Delgado stood aside as he too fingered Lia crudely, and she could not suppress the sigh that escaped her lips as his fingers probed her.

"I reckon you're right," he said. "The bitch is positively on heat."

"Let's get some heat into that arse of hers too," growled Chet.

"Good idea," said Delgado. "Four strokes each guys. That should teach her who's boss around here."

Lia watched with apprehension as Mex approached her. She knew she made the perfect target, her buttocks completely unprotected. She flinched as she felt Mex tap her there with the cane, taking aim. Then he drew it back.

Swish! Whack!

He brought the weapon down on her backside with all the strength he could muster, making her grunt with pain as it cut into her tender flesh. She saw the corporal lick his lips at the sight, and she knew he was enjoying the show.

Swish! Whack!

Down it came again, this time on the underside of her bottom cheeks, making her body sway forward with the force of the blow.

Swish! Whack!

"Ah!" she cried as the cane sliced across the top of her legs, leaving another read streak on her otherwise flawless flesh.

Swish! Whack!

Mex's final blow fell almost precisely where the first had, making the mark sting anew. Lia was breathing heavily, her backside on fire. She wondered if she could possibly survive a further four blows from the other two. She looked at her audience, their eyes fixed on her naked body, and she felt a sudden surge of excitement, the combination of bondage and pain bringing on the perverse pleasure she could never understand, but which was clearly deeply rooted inside her.

Delgado took the cane from Mex. He ran his eyes over her helpless body, a sly smile playing about his lips. "Such a lovely body," he murmured. "Especially those delectable tits. Let's see what they'd look like with a couple of stripes across them."

Lia was astounded. Surely he wasn't going to cane her breasts? Even Helda had not allowed that, though she had threatened it on a number of occasions and often slapped her there. She gave a sharp intake of breath as she felt him lay the weapon across her firm globes.

"Put your head up," he ordered. "Shoulders back. Present your tits to me."

Lia obeyed as best she could, thrusting her chest forward to allow him the target he required. She watched anxiously as he raised the cane in front of her face.

Thwack!

He slashed it hard across the top of her twin mounds, causing them to quiver deliciously. He used none of the force that Mex had, but still it left a cruel red stripe across her creamy flesh.

The blow had another effect though. Lia's nipples began to pucker and harden. She blushed as she realised what was happening, powerless to control her own body as her nipples swelled until they were solid and protruding, pointing stiffly outwards and upwards.

Delgado gave a snort. "Look at that, guys. I reckon she likes it." To illustrate the point he laid the cane across her nipples and it remained where it was, supported by the erect buds. Lia looked down at the weapon of punishment, wondering at the recalcitrance of her body.

Delgado held the cane again and once more took aim.

Thwack!

This time it struck across the front of Lia's breasts, catching her just above the nipples, marking her soft skin once again. She gave a little whimper as the stinging pain hit her, but at the same time she felt a spasm in her vagina.

Delgado reached down between her legs and felt the heat of her sex. He grinned knowingly at her. "Want some more?" he asked, shoving his fingers deeper into her so that she moaned aloud. "That's enough on your tits," he said. "After all, there's no sense damaging the merchandise."

He slid his fingers out and moved behind her. Once more she felt the tap on her glowing backside.

Swish! Whack!

This time he showed no restraint as he beat her arse, rocking her forward with the force of the blow.

Swish! Whack!

The next blow fell quickly, catching Lia unawares so that she gave a cry as it landed. Her backside was on fire and she wasn't sure she could stand the four blows still to come. Sweat was trickling down her naked flesh, making her glisten in the sunlight, and she was panting with arousal as she watched Chet take the cane from Delgado.

Swish! Whack!

Swish! Whack!

Swish! Whack!

Swish! Whack!

Chet's blows struck with such rapid succession that she barely had time to think. He struck her with deadly accuracy, leaving a row of four stripes in parallel lines across her buttocks, the first one still white even as the final one fell so that the men were able to watch them darken to red together. But at last her punishment was over, and she hung in her bonds, her backside and breasts striped with the cane's marks, her nipples hard and her sex wet, tell-tale moisture trickling down her thighs.

"OK," said Delgado, "cut her down."

The sergeant produced a knife from his belt, which sliced easily through Lia's bonds. She staggered slightly as her weight came back on her feet, but he caught her, one arm around her waist.

"You wanna fuck her?" asked Delgado.

The sergeant nodded.

"I guess that's OK by me."

Lia looked at him, wondering at the power he assumed over her, just casually giving her to the sergeant to be screwed. But the thought sent a new surge of lust through her as she realised how she loved to be dominated, to be tied up and punished, then turned over to a man whose name she did not even know.

The sergeant wasted no time, shoving her onto her back and opening his trousers. Lia licked her lips as his rod sprang into view, stiff and thick, a drop of pre-come at the tip. He knelt down between her legs and she instinctively spread them for him. He sprawled over her, his heavy body pressing down on her.

"Ah!" Lia cried out with delight as he shoved his cock into her, stabbing it home with force. He began fucking her, his hips pumping, taking her breath away as he forced himself down on her. Lia moaned and writhed under the onslaught, her body alive with unbridled passion, the arousal triggered by the beating spurring her to new heights.

The sergeant came quickly, his ejaculation catching her by surprise. His cock was still spitting creamy gobs of spunk when he pulled it out, spattering it over her belly. Lia gave a whimper of frustration as she realised he had finished. She was still burning with desire, writhing on the ground, her hips grinding. Then with a gasp of relief she realised the corporal was undoing his pants. He stood over her, his cock rising erect from his flies.

"You want it?" he asked.

"Y-yes, please."

"How bad?"

"Really bad... please fuck me. I really need it."

"Get on your hands and knees."

Lia did as she was ordered, scrambling over onto all fours. "Open your legs wide and push your tits down."

Lia obeyed, pressing her shoulders down so that her nipples brushed the ground, raising her striped arse to him and pushing back so that the pink lips of her sex lay open for him. She was barely in control, her hips moving back and forth as if against some imaginary lover.

The corporal delayed a little longer, enjoying the sight of the totally aroused girl, so anxious to be penetrated, her red arse beautifully presented. Then he knelt down, grasped her hips and thrust into her.

Lia gave a cry of joy as he impaled her on his stiff weapon and began fucking her. He too showed no finesse at all, treating her roughly, simply as a receptacle for his rampant cock. But Lia didn't care. This was how she loved to be fucked. Treated as no more than a pleasure object. It was a wonderful feeling to be owned and used, to be the plaything of anyone who wanted her, and she felt her orgasm build as her total wantonness filled her mind.

Like the sergeant the corporal did not last long, but this time Lia was ready for him, and as she felt him tense she let go, the force of her orgasm wracking her body as she thrashed about, screaming as a second helping of spunk pumped into her vagina.

She tightened her sex about him, milking his balls dry, holding him inside for as long as she was able to, and when he finally withdrew she flopped contentedly on the grass, semen oozing from her as she gazed up into the faces of her captors, a wistful smile of satisfaction on her lips.

Chapter 21

Once the men had satisfied their lusts in the young captive, Delgado, Mex and Chet set off through the forest once more. Lia rode in front of Delgado, her arms secured behind her back. She sat astride the forward part of the saddle, her sex pressed against the pommel, and as they rode her clitoris rubbed against the leather, keeping her constantly aroused. Her condition was made more acute by Delgado's habit of frequently feeling her up, rubbing her breasts to keep her nipples hard and occasionally penetrating her with his forefinger, so that by the time they had been going for an hour or more she was panting again, much to the amusement of the three.

They rode on, only stopping twice in the day to water the horses and eat a small meal. When night fell they halted and set up camp in the woods beside a river. The first thing Delgado did was to make sure Lia was secure, shackling her leg to a stout tree with a thick chain. It was long enough to allow her to wander and stretch her legs a little, but prevented any possibility of escape.

They lit a campfire and Delgado prepared a meal. After eating they made Lia wash the dishes in the river and pack them away while the men sat around the fire, talking, smoking and drinking. Once she had finished they summoned her over.

"Stand properly now," ordered Delgado.

Lia placed her hands behind her head and thrust her hips forward, her heart beating fast with anticipation. Delgado stretched his arm out and ran his fingers over her backside. She winced as he felt the tender weals.

"You really do look exquisite with stripes across your arse," he mused. "And as for the ones on your tits. Quite irresistible, don't you agree?"

"They sure are," said Mex. "Real cute."

"Come over here," ordered Chet.

Lia moved warily to him. He reached out a hand, running it up her inner thigh, his fingers lightly touching her skin. His hand rose higher, barely brushing her sex lips, but enough to make her draw breath sharply. He let his fingers stray further until they found the underside of a breast. They paused momentarily, Lia hardly daring to breathe. For one so powerfully built Chet was remarkably gentle, and despite her reluctance her flesh tingled with anticipation as she waited for his hand to move again.

His palm closed over her breast and caressed it. "Very nice," he murmured.

"Come on Chet," called Mex impatiently. "You gonna fuck her? If not pass her over here."

Lia's stomach turned over. It was not just what was said, it was the casual way the words were spoken. She was simply a slave to their whims, a realisation that sent a powerful spasm of arousal through her.

Chet took her there and then, stretched on her back by the fire, gasping and moaning as he filled her with his stiff cock. Once he had deposited his seed into her Mex took over. He draped her face down across one of the saddles and took her from behind, his heavy thrusts making her grunt with every stroke - grunts that turned into cries of encouragement as she felt his sperm pump into her.

Finally it was Delgado's turn. He made her suck him, kneeling in the dust and slurping at his cock whilst wanking the shaft vigorously until he shot his load down her throat.

Before retiring for the night they hammered four stakes into the ground and chained her spread-eagled. Surprisingly she slept, exhausted by the rigours of the day, but she was woken at first light by Mex, who crawled onto her whilst still tethered and screwed her, followed by Chet and Delgado. Lia, as usual, responded enthusiastically to the treatment, the bondage heightening her enjoyment, her orgasms loud and long.

At last they freed her arms and legs and she was allowed to bathe, her leg iron still in place, while Delgado prepared the breakfast. Then they were off once more, winding their way through the forest.

It was nearly midday when Delgado reined his horse to a halt at the top of a ridge. Below Lia could see a farmhouse, with a number of outbuildings, and a track that led away through the trees. They began to pick their way down towards it. The path was steep and narrow, and Lia feared the horses would slip and fall, but they were sure-footed beasts and carried the four of them safely to the bottom. Once on the flat Delgado spurred his horse on toward the farmhouse.

The buildings were old and dilapidated and Lia thought they must be deserted, but as they pulled the horses up a door swung open in the farmhouse and a man emerged. He was really old, but he eyed Lia up with some interest.

"You're late," he said. "You said you'd be back yesterday."

"A bit of a problem with this young lady," said Delgado. "Don't worry, we'll pay for the extra day."

"Darned right you will," grumbled the man. "You wanna eat something? I got a stew on the stove."

"That'd be good," said Delgado. "Where do you want the horses?"

"Just leave them in the yard here. I'll see to them later."

The men dismounted, along with Lia. Delgado pulled the leg iron from his saddlebag and secured her to the same post as the one to which the horses were tied. "Now stand properly," he said.

Lia took up her submissive stance, much to the delight of the old man, who was unable to take his eyes off her. But the men trooped into the house, leaving her alone.

A while passed, then the door opened again. The old man emerged, carrying a bowl of stew. He looked her up and down, his eyes wide. Lia blushed, but did not move. The man approached her hesitantly, holding out the stew. Lia made no move at first, until he gave a nod of his head. She reached out and took the food. The man turned and went back inside the house.

Lia ate hungrily, scooping the food into her mouth with a spoon. The ride had made her hungry and the stew tasted good. Soon she was holding an empty bowl, and placed it on the ground, then clasped her hands behind her head and waited.

The man returned. He went to pick up the bowl, then paused, his eyes fixed on Lia's breasts. He reached out a hand, running a bony old finger along the stripes that adorned them. Lia closed her eyes at the touch.

"Who gave you these?" the man asked.

"They did," she said, nodding towards the farmhouse.

"How come?"

"Because I tried to escape."

"So they beat your tits?"

"Yes. And my bum."

"Your arse as well?"

"Yes."

"Show me."

Lia turned around so he could see the marks on her backside. He gave a low whistle.

"Can I touch?"

"If you want to." Lia felt the man's fingers tracing the marks of her beating.

"Tell me about how they did this to you," he said, and she told him how she had been tied, and the three men took it in turns to cane her. The old timer listened, his eyes wide, his fingers running back and forth over Lia's bare buttocks.

"What happened next?" he asked, when she had finished.

"Nothing."

"Come on, girlie. You're not trying to tell me they just cut you down." As he spoke he slipped his finger down the crack of her bum, and felt her wetness."

"N-no," she stammered.

"Tell me then."

Lia went on to tell how she had been fucked by the two security guards. But the man wanted more, so she was forced to recount her night in camp. And all the time his coarse old fingers were rubbing back and forth over her sex.

"What the hell are you up to now?"

Delgado's voice made Lia start. She hadn't heard the three men emerge from the farmhouse. Suddenly she realised what a sight she must make. Almost subconsciously she had bent herself forward over the hitching post, her backside shoved up and back to allow the man unrestricted access to her vagina, her breasts hanging and quivering under his touch. She snatched her body erect and placed her hands behind her head, but the old man continued to finger her, apparently unconcerned by the presence of the others.

"She's certainly a horny little bitch, isn't she?" he said.

Delgado laughed. "She just loves it. That's why she goes around bare-arsed like that. No need to waste time stripping off. Still, we gotta get going."

The old man withdrew his fingers from Lia's sex, wiping the moisture off on her thigh, leaving two glistening streaks there. As he did so there came the sound of an engine starting, and a few seconds later an old van emerged from one of the barns with Mex at the wheel. It was battered and rusting, but the engine still ran and with a squeak of brakes it halted beside Lia. Delgado pulled two sets of cuffs from his bag, and once again she found her wrists and elbows secured. Then he pushed her into the van.

"In the back," he ordered.

Lia climbed awkwardly over the seats into the rear of the vehicle. Inside it smelt musty and greasy, but an old piece of carpet had been laid on the floor, which was at least fairly clean. She sat with her back to the side of the van, and her cuffs were undone momentarily, then slipped through a metal handle set into the floor. Once she was secure the three men climbed in the front, and with a grinding of gears they were on the move once more.

Chapter 22

The first part of the journey was really bumpy as the old van rattled along the farm track, and Lia found it quite difficult to maintain her balance. All she had was the handle to which her wrists were attached and she clung to it grimly, trying to keep herself upright. In the front the three men chatted idly, apparently unconcerned about the discomfort of their passenger. Then the van hit a particularly large bump and Lia lurched forward. There was a bang, and she realised she was no longer secured to the handle. Its attachment points had been so rusted that the weight of her body was too much and one of them gave way, allowing her cuffs to slip out. She glanced fearfully at the men in the front, wondering if they had heard or seen anything, but they showed no signs of having done so. She braced herself against the side of the van, her heart beating fast. For the first time since she'd been recaptured the possibility of escape was a reality.

At last the van swung to the left and the bumping and lurching stopped. They had reached the highway, and Lia was able to relax as the vehicle gained speed. They travelled for another hour or so along the highway, and from her position in the rear she could see almost nothing, but occasionally she would hear a roar as a truck thundered past, so she guessed they must be on one of the major trunk roads.

Eventually she realised they were slowing. She felt the vehicle swing off the main road and stop for a few seconds, then move forward again, but this time much slower. She guessed they had turned into a service area, possibly even the same one that the Bikers had taken her when she was first captured. The van came to a halt and Mex jerked on the handbrake and cut the engine. The three men turned to their naked captive, who was as they had left her, arms secure. She prayed they would not check her bonds.

"Time for a little refreshment," said Delgado. "I take it you're not coming in with us?"

Lia said nothing, but her thoughts went to the last time she had visited such a place. This time she wanted to be left outside.

"Right," said Delgado, "we're gonna have a couple of beers. But first we've got a call to make. Helda's gonna be pretty pleased when she finds her little whore is back in harness. I reckon she can be here in less than an hour. Then we're going to have to part company, I'm afraid."

Again Lia did not reply, but her thoughts were racing. Helda less than an hour away? She had to get as far as possible from this place. But how?

To her relief her three captors climbed out of the van without checking her bonds, simply slamming the door and leaving her alone. She stayed where she was for a full five minutes, not daring to move. Then, when at last she felt the coast was clear, she got gingerly to her knees and shuffled forward. She leaned over the front seats and stared out. They were in one of the service areas. On one side was the diner, with its neon signs flashing on and off, advertising its wares, and on the other was the refuelling area, where the mighty trucks drew up to refill their tanks.

As Lia watched one of them pulled away from the pumps and headed towards the van. Instinctively she ducked down, not wishing to be seen by the drivers. The truck stopped about fifty yards from where the van was parked, and for a second she wondered if she had been spotted. The two men descended from the cab, but instead of heading in her direction they disappeared into a small brick building.

Lia continued her vigil, waiting to see what would happen next. The men were gone for about two minutes, then they emerged together and climbed back into the cab. There was a roar from the engine, a plume of black smoke from the great chrome exhaust and the vehicle was moving again, heading for the exit.

Lia watched as a second truck pulled away from the pumps and was surprised to see that it too halted by the building and the men went inside. The same happened with the third to leave. Then she realised the little building was a toilet, and that the men were taking the opportunity to relieve themselves before setting out on the open road. She watched three more trucks pass. Two of the three stopped by the toilet block. This had to be her best means of escape; she had to conceal herself in a truck while the men were taking a piss.

But first of all she had to cover fifty yards across the car park, in broad daylight, stark naked with her hands tethered behind her. She scanned the parking area. There was a scattering of vans and trucks between her and the lavatory block. It wasn't much, but it was all the cover she had, and time was fast running out. She took a deep breath. She had to try it.

She climbed over onto the front seats, then fumbled with the door handle on the driver's side. It wasn't easy with her hands tethered as they were, but eventually she managed and the door opened a crack. She checked out the windscreen. Two men were making their way across the parking lot to the diner. She waited until they were safely inside, then pushed the door open and stepped down onto the tarmac. It felt hot under her bare feet, and gravel dug into her, but she pushed the pain from her mind.

Her first objective was another van about ten yards away, and she scuttled across the open space as quickly as she was able, crouching down beside it. She made sure the coast was clear, then made a dash for a large truck some fifteen yards beyond. She had burned her bridges well and truly, and she had to go on. She felt dreadfully exposed, leaning against the side of the truck. Her eyes darted about, fearful that she might be spotted.

She made her way down the length of the truck and peered round the back. She froze. A group of four men had emerged from the diner and were heading towards her. She crouched down and slid beneath the trailer, where she remained, her heart pounding, praying the men would veer from the route they were taking, but still they came on, so close now she could hear their voices. She moved behind one of the massive sets of wheels on the truck, then kept perfectly still. Two of the men were no more than a couple of yards away now and as they came alongside they stopped.

"You wanna check the load?" said one.

"Why, is there a problem?"

"Not specially. It's just about time we checked it."

"Nah. It'll be OK."

Lia gave a sigh of relief as the two men moved on. She heard the doors bang as they climbed into the cab. She was in a quandary. She knew that the truck would move away, leaving her exposed. She looked out in the direction of the lavatory. There was another truck less than ten yards away. She would have to get to it.

Suddenly she saw something that made her give a stifled cry of dismay. There were two men sitting in its cab. They must be the other two of the foursome, and she knew that the moment she broke into the open they would see her.

Then the engine of the truck under whose trailer she was hiding burst into life. If it moved away now she would be left in full view of the one behind. She cursed her luck and watched the other cab anxiously. The men inside were chatting and showed no signs of moving. If they saw her they would certainly take her back to the diner, then all would be lost.

The truck's engine continued to rumble, but still it did not move off. Lia was helpless. All she could do was watch the other cab, and hope.

Suddenly a plume of smoke bellowed from the exhaust of the second truck and she heard its engine start. Her heart leapt. Maybe there was still hope. She watched the vehicle, willing it to move, but it remained where it was. Through the windscreen she could discern the crew, still chatting. At the same moment she heard the sound of the gears being engaged on the vehicle under which she was hiding. Then the engine note began to rise and all seemed lost. She held her breath and waited for the exposure and capture that must inevitably follow.

But with a gasp of relief she saw the other truck begin to move, swinging out and passing the one she was hiding under, which began to move too. She crouched lower as the trailer passed over her, then she was in the open and on her feet, running for all she was worth, her thrusting breasts bouncing as she sped across the tarmac. There was a truck pulled up beside the latrine, its doors open, and Lia made the decision to go straight for it. She sprinted, watching the door of the low building, hoping desperately that the men would not emerge just yet. It seemed to take forever to reach the throbbing vehicle, but at last she was there.

There was no point checking to make sure she hadn't been spotted. It was now or never. The first step up to the cab was high, and without the ability to grasp the handle that ran up the side it was extremely difficult to climb onto. She placed her foot on it and leapt upwards, only to drop back again. She tried a second time with similar results. Lia gave a sob of despair. At any moment the men would return, or someone else would spot her. It was a miracle nobody had seen her so far. She placed her foot on the step once more, and with a superhuman effort managed to jump up, so she was standing on it.

She climbed on, a trifle unsteadily, going up step by step until at last she was level with the open door. She fell through onto the seats. At once she was upright. Behind and above the seats was a bunk bed, and she climbed onto it, rolling over the plastic surface as far as she could, then lying still, hardly daring to breathe.

Almost at once she felt the cab move as the driver and his mate mounted the steps. The doors slammed, and with a jolt they were moving. They travelled at low speed for about half a minute, then they stopped again. For a moment Lia thought the game was up, then she realised with relief that it was just the checkpoint at the gate. They were stationary for only a few seconds, before she felt the vehicle lurch and they were off on the highway.

Chapter 23

The truck roared on, gathering speed all the time. Lia remained where she was, her heart still beating fast after her amazing escape. The driver and his mate clearly had no idea she was aboard, and she could hear them conversing idly below. Soon even the talk died away and they turned on the radio. The strains of country and western drifted up to where she hid, and she closed her eyes. Before long she was asleep.

She was woken by the sense of the vehicle slowing. Although she could not see out, the reflection of the headlights on the ceiling of the cab told her it was dark. She lay listening as the vehicle came to a halt. One of the doors to the cab opened, and someone got out. There was a clank of chains, and they moved forward. Then she heard the bang of a large gate being shut. They were in some kind of enclosure, probably stopping for the night; most of the hauliers maintained a number of stopping places, since it was unsafe to park on the roadsides.

The truck swung round and came to a halt, and the engine died. The silence was very welcome after the constant drone of the diesel, but Lia had to hold her breath for fear the men would hear her.

The driver's door opened, then slammed, and she knew she was alone. Nevertheless she waited a few minutes before sliding to the edge of the bunk and peering over. There was nobody in the cab. Carefully she climbed down onto the seats and glanced out the windscreen. The truck was on the edge of a wide parking area, and she could see a heavy chain fence, with the highway beyond. She wondered what to do. Despite the fact she had escaped from Delgado, she was clearly not safe. Apart from anything else she was trussed, her arms pinned behind her. If only there was someone she could rely on. Someone who could contact Thorkil, so he could rescue her. She considered remaining in the cab, but to do so would mean certain discovery eventually. There was nothing else for it; she would have to get out.

As with the van earlier, operating the door handle was no easy feat, but eventually she managed it. She eased herself backwards onto the steps and climbed down carefully, jumping from the bottom one to land on hard gravel. Once she had steadied herself she pressed her body against the trailer and inched along its length, peering round to see where she was. The enclosure was quite small, only a hundred or so yards across. It consisted of an open parking area, with a small building at one end. She could see a light burning inside and a plume of smoke rose from the chimney. There were two more trucks parked on the far side of the enclosure, and nothing else.

Lia studied the fence. It was more than twelve feet high. There was no way she could climb it with her arms secured. She had to free herself. She wondered if the truck was carrying tools that could be used to cut through the cuffs. She went to the rear doors, turned her back and fumbled for the handle.

A light shone in her face. "What the hell do you think you're doing?"

Lia could not see the man behind the powerful flashlight as she blinked into its beam. She cursed herself for being so careless. She should have known that someone would be on watch, despite the security of the enclosure. She remained where she was, like a frightened rabbit.

"I said, what are you doing?"

"I - I was looking for some tools."

"Some what?"

"Some tools."

"Well you won't find any in there. He's hauling cigarettes. What do you want tools for?"

"My hands. They're tied."

"Show me."

Slowly Lia turned round, revealing the cuffs to the man. "I see what you mean," he said. "Who did that to you?"

"Some men. They were kidnapping me."

"And they stripped you as well?"

"I was already naked."

"I see. But how the hell did you get in here?"

"I came in this truck."

"What, Buck and Dan brought you?"

"I don't know their names. I stowed away. I was trying to escape."

"Hmm," he scratched his head. "I guess you'd better come inside. I'm sure the boys will be pleased to meet you."

"Please, couldn't you just let me out?" she pleaded.

"What, onto the highway? In that state?"

"I - I just want to get away."

"No chance, baby. You're coming with me."

The man took her by the arm and led her towards the building. Lia tried to hang back but he was strong and pulled her along. As he reached for the handle of the door she felt a pang of apprehension, only too aware of her vulnerability. The door flew open and the man pushed her inside. The room was warm but smoky, an aroma of food hanging in the air. Opposite the door was a table, at which five men were sitting, playing cards.

"Look what I've found."

The five swung round and their eyes widened. Lia felt the blood rush to her cheeks as they studied her, forced to remain where she was as they feasted their eyes on her breasts and her shaven sex.

"Wow!"

"What a beauty."

"Where did you find that?"

"She was outside, sneaking about the back of the trucks. Claimed she stowed away in Buck and Dan's cab."

"Our cab?" The man was large and burly, his hair cut short. On his hairy arms were tattoos of naked women. "Where the fuck were you?" he

100

demanded.

"On the bunk," said Lia timidly. "I got in at the service depot. I was trying to escape from someone, you see."

"Damn, Buck, that means we've had her trussed up like that in the cab all afternoon, and we didn't even know it!" He was younger than the first, and thinner, with long hair and a ring through his nose. If the other one was Buck, Lia figured, he must be Dan.

"Talk about a missed opportunity," said another of the men, laughing. Dan shot him an angry glance.

"But the question is, what do we do with her?"

"Well let me know when you decide," said the man with the flashlight. "I'd better get back outside."

He left Lia standing just inside the door. She stared apprehensively from face to face, wondering what they would do with her. She wished her hands were free, so at least she could cover herself with them.

For a few moments there was silence, then Buck rose and crossed to where she stood. "Where were you headed?" he asked.

"I want to get to depot twenty-nine," she said.

"Twenty-nine, eh? Why?"

"There's someone there. A Biker. I'm a Biker's girl."

"I should have guessed from those stripes across your tits. They know how treat a girl, do Bikers. Have you had your arse thrashed too?"

She dropped her eyes. "Yes."

"Show us."

Slowly Lia turned and raised her arms as best she could to reveal the marks of her punishment, crisscrossing her rear. She could have explained that it was Delgado and not a Biker who put them there, but there didn't seem much point.

"Very nice," said Buck. "Very nice indeed. Don't you agree, boys?"

The others nodded. Then Buck said something unexpected.

"You're heading for twenty-nine, aren't you, Slim?" The words were addressed to a tall man, who had sat silent until now, watching proceedings. He nodded.

"Fancy a passenger?"

"What's it worth?"

Buck turned to Lia. "Passengers don't travel for free with Slim, you know. He'll want something in return. What you offering?"

Lia's stomach gave a little lurch. The question made her more aware than ever of her naked and helpless state. She knew what was being asked of her, and she was shocked at how her body was responding. She dropped her eyes, aware that her nipples had hardened. Then she looked up again at Buck. She did not speak. She did not have to. The gesture said it all. She was offering all she had. Prostituting herself for the sake of a lift. Her cheeks glowed as she considered her wantonness, and at the same time she felt the thrill of arousal creep into her loins.

Buck placed a hand on her breast, squeezing it gently. "We get the message," he said. "And you get the ride. In more ways than one."

"Let's fuck her now," said Dan, enthused. "Come on, who's first?"

"Yeah," said another, "c'mon. I wanna be first."

He and Dan rose and began to converge on Lia. Dan grabbed her breasts. Lia tried to take a step back, but she was already against the door. They pinned her against it, reaching for her crotch. She gasped as a finger penetrated her, while another was running down the crack of her bum. A mouth closed over her nipple and she found herself being pushed and shoved back and forth as the two men fought over her. She began to feel the first stages of panic rising in her as they licked and groped. She tried to struggle, but to no avail. They were too strong for her.

"Stop!"

The sudden shout caught the two men by surprise and they froze instantly. Lia shook herself free of them, staggering across the room. She turned to look at Slim, who was on his feet.

"Stop fighting over her like a couple of mutts over a bitch," he rapped. "The lady's not going anywhere, is she?"

"Sorry Slim," mumbled the pair.

"Anyhow," said Slim, a wily smile on his lips, "I've got a much better idea. Instead of fighting over who's gonna be first, we can all be first."

The others stared at him. "All?" said Buck.

"Sure. I used to know a whore down south who claimed she could take on five men at once."

"Five?"

"So she said. Never tried it myself, but I always intended to. Let's see how this little lady gets on."

"Yeah, sure. I'm game."

"First of all we gotta get those shackles off her. Len, go and get some cutters."

"Sure thing," said the one who'd been mauling her with Dan. He shoved the door open and set off at a trot.

Lia stayed silent, her eyes going from man to man. All five? They wanted her to take on all five? Her mind went through the possible combinations, and she felt the wetness inside her increase as the ideas tumbled through her brain.

Buck and Dan moved a bench from one side of the room. It was wide and heavily padded. The fifth man stirred himself too. He was another driver. His name was Jack and it had been his sidekick who found Lia in the first place.

By the time the bench was in place Len had returned with a pair of cutters. They were big, with long handles and strong jaws. Buck made her face the wall while he slipped the blade under her cuffs. There was a loud snap and one fell away from her wrist. He moved to the other wrist and quickly she was revelling in her newfound freedom, the men watching her expectantly.

Slim loosened his belt and opened his pants. His cock was already stiff and Lia stared at it with undisguised interest. He lay back on the bench, then beckoned to her. She moved forward hesitantly, her heart beating wildly. Her knees trembled slightly as she approached him, but she wasn't sure if it was fear or lust that made them shake. She straddled him and the bench, positioned just above his jutting weapon. He nodded to her, and she began to lower herself onto him.

She shivered as she felt the tip of his cock touch her sex. She took it in her hands and guided it into herself. She was extremely wet, and he slipped into her easily. She let herself crouch lower and lower, until he was all the way inside her. He filled her wonderfully, stretching the walls of her vagina and plundering deep inside her. When settled astride him he pulled her forward, down until she was lying on him, her legs stretched wide, her feet barely touching the floor.

Lia felt an odd sensation on her bottom. Something cold was trickling down the valley between her buttocks. She craned her neck round to see Buck standing there. He had a small bottle of oil in his hand and was rubbing it into her anus, his fingers slipping inside her, the sensation both strange and erotic, particularly since her vagina was so full of cock. She dropped her eyes to his groin. Buck's cock was standing proud from his fly, and shining with oil.

He positioned himself behind her, the tip of his weapon rubbing up and down between the cheeks of her backside. Lia tried as best she could to relax the muscles of her sphincter. Only once before had she been fucked in the anus, by one of the Black Cat's clients, and it was painful, at first.

Buck began pressing his rampant organ against her tight rear hole, twisting it to facilitate the penetration. Lia gave a cry as it suddenly surged into her, stretching the muscles of her rear passage as it did so. This time there was none of the pain, just the perverse thrill of being double penetrated, of opening her body to admit two men at once. She felt the rough curls of Buck's pubic hair against her flesh, and she knew he was all the way inside. Neither man made a movement. Then a hand grasped her hair and her head was pulled round, and there, just at the level of her mouth, stood Dan's cock. It bobbed up and down before her eyes, the glans exposed and shining. She opened her mouth and took it inside. At the same moment she felt her wrists grabbed from either side and guided to the shafts of two more swollen penises.

Lia's body was alive with arousal. She was filled by rock-hard cocks, while she held two more in her hands. She was going to pleasure five men at once, and the idea sent a new surge of moisture rushing through her sex.

Slim's first thrust was a cue to his companions, and she felt Buck's cock shove in her backside, whilst Dan began ramming his hips forward, his youthful exuberance returning as he fucked Lia's face. She tightened her grip on the two shafts in her hands and began to wank them vigorously, making the two men grunt with enjoyment. She could not believe what was happening to her. But for the mouthful of male flesh pumping into her mouth she would have cried aloud with bliss. Her body was being battered back and forth by Slim and Buck, and it was all she could do to hold her head steady as she slurped greedily on Dan's organ. It seemed impossible to establish a rhythm, and in the end she gave up, lying passively sandwiched between them, concentrating on the cocks in her hands and abandoning her body to the other three.

The first to come was Buck, his hot semen spurting into her rectum as he cursed with pleasure, the pulsations of his cock sending waves of pleasure through Lia's ravaged body as she accepted his seed in so intimate a place. Seconds later it was Dan's turn, his cock unleashing copious amounts of spunk into her mouth and over her face. Lia spluttered and gasped as she tried her best to swallow the glutinous unguent. Slim then unleashed a stream of semen deep inside her cunt with a hoarse grunt of satisfaction. She could feel Buck withdrawing from her arse, a dribble of warm sperm escaping from her rear passage as she vigorously wanked the other two.

She was roughly pulled off Slim, and she lost grip of the two cocks as they dragged her to the table and lay her back across it with her backside projected over the edge. She peered down between her breasts and watched as Jack yanked her legs apart, staring down at her open slit before plunging his stiff prick into her, making her cry out as she was penetrated yet again. As Jack began to fuck her Len climbed onto the table and sat astride her midriff.

"Squeeze your tits together," he ordered. "I want to fuck your tits. Do as I tell you."

Lia cupped her breasts and watched as he positioned his stiff cock in the valley between them, then pressed them together so the erect nipples were almost touching. Len began to move his hips back and forth, his cock trapped between her tits, his face a picture of contentment as he fucked her cleavage. She felt her climax rising, spurred on by the taste of spunk in her mouth and the sensation of it deep in her cunt and trickling from her anus. Jack was fucking hard, and though she could not see his face she knew he was close to coming, and this time when her cunt was filled she responded with her own orgasm, her cries ringing about the room as she let herself go. Then just as she was beginning to come down Len unleashed a stream of semen onto her face, neck and breasts. She opened her mouth, endeavouring to catch and swallow the sticky gobs that burst from his cock, and a second orgasm swept through her as she felt Len ejaculating all over her throat and swollen breasts.

By the time he climbed off her she knew she must look a sight, her face, hair, neck and breasts coated with spunk, her sex open, more spunk leaking from it. She gazed round at the men, panting with the force of her orgasms.

All at once there was a commotion outside. Shouts rang out and the roar of a motorcycle could be heard. The men turned and stared at the door, just as it crashed open.

A figure stood framed in the doorway; a Biker wearing black leathers studded with silver. Cold eyes darted around the room, then alighted on the naked girl spread out on the bench.

"Still up to your old tricks, I see," said Helda.

Chapter 24

Lia stood on the table, her hands clasped behind her head, her legs spread, looking down at the faces below her. The truckers had retreated to the back of the room, and were gathered in a huddle looking very uncomfortable. There were six Bikers besides Helda, some of whom Lia recognised from her days at the Black Cat. Delgado was there too, his face a picture of relief. It was clear to Lia that Helda had not been at all pleased to find she had escaped, and there was little doubt that Delgado would have been severely punished had she not been found.

But she had been found. Somehow they had tracked her down, and now she was back in Helda's clutches. She trembled at the feel of the leather tip of Helda's whip brushing her flesh as the Biker walked round her young captive. Lia's body was still spattered with the drivers' sperm, now cold on her bare flesh. She knew there were sticky patches on her cheeks and chin, and longed to wipe them off. But for the moment she was not daring to move as her captor examined her.

"Well, my dear," said Helda, in a menacing tone, "you have led us a merry dance, haven't you?"

Lia said nothing, staring straight ahead, her pulse racing.

"And you very nearly gave us the slip again today," Helda went on. "It was most fortunate for Delgado here that a young man at the refuelling bay saw you climb into that truck. It had to be you. After all, who else prances about in service areas in broad daylight whilst utterly naked? It took us a while to find a witness to your escape, but he told us all we needed to know. Then it was just a case of finding this little enclosure. But I see you haven't been idle. How many of these truckers managed to fuck you before we arrived?"

"Five of them," muttered Lia, her eyes downcast.

"Five? In your cunt? I would have thought that was fast going, even for you. Tell us how you managed it."

Lia said nothing.

Thwack!

Helda's whip swatted Lia's right buttock, making her stagger. "Tell us!"

"Only two in my cunt."

"And the rest?"

"One between my breasts, one in my mouth. And one..." Lia's voice trailed away.

"Yes?"

"In my bottom."

"Your arse? He fucked your arse? Show me. Bend down and show me."

Lia bent forward. She took her hands from behind her head and used them to pull the cheeks of her backside apart, her face glowing while Helda felt her anus. The touch made her sphincter contract, and she felt a trickle of semen escape and dribble down her leg.

"Fascinating," said Helda. "Maybe we should sell that orifice more often. There are plenty of men who prefer the tightness of a woman's arse. Stand up."

Lia straightened, and replaced her hands.

"Is there a shower in this place?" Helda asked the truckers.

"Through there," muttered Buck, indicating a door at the end of the room.

"Well I think it's time you got cleaned up, young lady. We have to be going. And don't even think of escaping. A couple of my guards will accompany you inside. I think they'd enjoy that. Now move!"

Lia scrambled down from the table, two burly Bikers just behind her. She pushed open the door and found herself in a spartan washroom, with an old shower at one side; a pipe that rose up from the floor with a broad shower head on the top. Halfway up the pipe was a dull chrome tap. There was no curtain, but Lia doubted she would have been allowed to use one anyway. The two Bikers leant against the wall, watching her as she struggled with the tap. The cold water cascaded in a rush, catching her by surprise, taking her breath away. There was a piece of soap on a rack on the wall, and she began to wash herself, sluicing the men's dried seed from her flesh, soaping her breasts and tummy, then allowing the icy water to wash it away.

After scrubbing every part of her body she turned off the tap. There was no towel, so she stepped wet onto the cold floor, her body covered with tiny goose-pimples, her nipples hard. Suddenly she felt her arms gripped from behind, her shoulders pinned back so that her breasts were thrust forward. While one Biker held her the other began feeling her up, clutching her breasts and rubbing them, running a hand up her thigh and penetrating her sex with his finger. Lia tried to struggle but she was held firm as the man's fingers began to stimulate her. And she could feel the hardness of the other Biker's cock pressing into her hip.

"Jeez, it's true what they say about her," said the one fingering her. "I've never known a girl come to the boil so quickly."

"You reckon there's time?" said his companion.

"Nah, she'd only have to shower again." He tweaked Lia's nipple between finger and thumb. "Some other time, eh baby?" he said, and with a final thrust into her vagina he removed his fingers, leaving Lia panting for breath.

They opened the door and led her out. The truckers were still standing in an isolated group, whilst Helda perched on the table. There was a powerful sexuality about the lady Biker, in her tight leather outfit, her full breasts pressing against the jacket, which was open almost to the waist, revealing a large portion of her ample breasts. Her pants were skin-tight, showing off the contours of her long slim legs beautifully. Her boots were black and shiny, with high heels and silver spurs. She rose cat-like to her feet as Lia entered.

"Hmm, that's a little better," she purred. "Quite delightful, really. I'm almost tempted to have you myself. I'm sure you're a real accomplished cunt licker."

The words gave Lia an odd sensation in her stomach. Helda was extremely attractive, and the thought of having her naked was one that appealed to her.

"All set to go then?" asked Helda, then suddenly snatched Lia's hair, pulling her roughly forward so that the unsuspecting girl stumbled against the table. Helda forced her down over it.

Thwack! Thwack! Thwack! Thwack! Thwack! Thwack!

She lashed Lia's arse with her whip, the strokes falling in quick succession, the hapless girl with no chance to protect herself, yelping with pain and surprise as the blows rained down.

Six blows. Then she stopped. She was panting with the exertion as she looked down at her captive, who writhed with the pain that coursed through her burning buttocks. The Biker grabbed her hair again and pulled her head round to face her, her eyes like thunder.

"Don't ever try to escape from me again," she growled, "or I'll lock you away where you'll never see the light of day again."

She released Lia, who staggered backwards, shocked by the vehemence of the woman.

"Get her outside," barked Helda. "We're leaving."

Chapter 25

Lia found it hard to think straight as she roared along the highway on the back of Helda's bike. Her ankles were shackled to the footrests and her hands trapped behind her by two metal cuffs at the rear of the seat. Her mind was numb. Too numb even to cry. After all that had happened to her she was back in Helda's hands again, with little or no chance of escape. And she had seemed so close. If only she had not fallen asleep on the Countess's land the guards would probably not have found her. She wondered what the Countess had thought; whether she suspected that Lia had been abducted, or whether she believed she had run away. Had she called Thorkil? She really hoped she had. At least it would be some kind of contact between them.

And then there were the truckers. They would have taken her to depot twenty-nine, and to Thorkil. She would have had to endure their treatment of her on the way, but that would have been small price to pay for her return to her true master.

But in the end it was Helda who won. She would never risk Lia escaping again.

The bikes sped on through the night, the other Bikers flanking Helda, using up the full width of the highway. Only Bikers would have dared to travel at night along these roads. The journey seemed to go on forever, the roar of the motorcycle engine and the rush of wind in her ears blotting out all other sounds, so that she felt deprived of her senses, almost as if in a dream.

Perhaps she had dozed. She wasn't sure. But suddenly she was aware of the Bikers slowing. She had absolutely no idea where she was. All around was dark, and there was no sign of any life. They pulled off the highway onto a long straight road. Despite the gloom Lia could see they were out of the forest. The land was flat and almost devoid of vegetation. She spotted a light ahead. At first she couldn't make out what it was. Then she saw that a barrier had been lowered across the road, and realised it was a checkpoint. On either side was a high fence, not unlike those that surrounded the depots, but taller and stronger looking.

The barrier was manned by men in uniform, who drew pistols from holsters as the bikes approached. Helda slowed right down and seemed about to stop, but as they came closer the men recognised her and there was a scramble to clear the road and raise the barrier. They achieved it just in time, and Helda and her entourage swept through, giving barely a glance to the guards.

They passed two more checkpoints, and had a similar reception at each. Clearly whatever the men were supposed to be guarding against it was not Helda.

Soon after they passed the final barrier a huge building loomed into view. It was like some kind of giant fortress, with turreted walls and watchtowers. The entire area about the building was lit by powerful floodlights, and the pencil beams of searchlights raked back and forth across the grounds. The Bikers sped along the length of the edifice, then swung round and came to a halt before a great double door, also bathed in light, with a sign across its top: *Bleakmoor Prison.*

Ever since the breakdown of law and order the authorities had struggled to retain some semblance of control over the people. In many cases, particularly in the cities, vigilante squads would roam the streets, meting out swift justice to anyone failing to defer to their authority. The Bikers ran large sections of the cities, though it was in the countryside that their influence was strongest. In all cases the security forces played a secondary role, generally acting with the consent of the Bikers.

The prisons remained, though. Many were used for housing the political opponents of the government, or anyone who wrote or spoke out against the authority of the ruling group. But there was still a need to incarcerate those less pleasant members of the criminal classes who threw themselves at the mercy of the authorities in order to escape the summary justice of the unofficial forces. These were the hardened criminals. The terrorists, armed robbers, and murderers.

The regimes in these prisons were severe. All attempts at rehabilitation had long since been abandoned. Nowadays they were ruled with an iron fist, and the order of the day was generally breaking stones or digging trenches. Lia stared up at the imposing face of the building. Why had they brought her here? And how was it that Helda was able to ride through the checkpoints with such ease?

Helda propped the machine on its stand and walked across to the great doors, and a smaller door set into one of the main ones opened, a man stepping out.

"Yes Madam?" he said deferentially.

"Tell the governor I want to see him," Helda said shortly.

The man disappeared back inside and Helda turned to her companions. "Bring her," she ordered.

Two of the men released Lia's ankles and freed her wrists from the seat, leaving them still fastened behind her. Then they led her into the prison, the other Bikers and Delgado remaining behind with their machines.

Lia felt really self-conscious as she was taken into the great building. All about were male guards, who regarded her naked body frankly, some giving wolf whistles as she passed. She did her best to ignore them, staring straight ahead as she padded over the cold stone floors. Helda seemed to know exactly where she was going, leading the way down dark corridors and up stone steps, penetrating ever deeper into the building.

At last they came to a door marked *Governor*. Helda shoved it open and stepped inside.

The office was in stark contrast to the rest of the building. The carpet on the floor was thick and the walls were hung with oil paintings. There was a desk at one end with a large imposing chair behind it. Helda strolled across and sat on it, placing her boots on the desk. She nodded to the escorts to undo Lia's cuffs, then they dragged her to the desk.

Lia spotted the manacles hanging down from the ceiling, looking strangely out of place in the comfortable room. The two Bikers made her lift her arms while they clamped her wrists, then they pulled on a chain and raised her arms above her head. Lia caught sight of her reflection in a mirror, probably placed there for just such a purpose; so any alleged miscreant standing on that spot could see themselves and ponder their fate.

The door suddenly opened, making Lia start. She glanced over her shoulder at the man who came in. He was not very tall, with a balding head and glasses. From his appearance he had obviously dressed in a hurry; his tie askew and one shirttail outside his trousers. He stared open-mouthed at the view of Lia's arse, and her face glowed as he took in the marks of the cane.

"Ah, Governor," said Helda. "So good of you to come." She made no effort to rise from his chair.

"It's always a pleasure to see you, Miss Helda," he said nervously.

"Good. And how are those two I brought in last week?"

"Back in solitary confinement. You did an excellent job, catching them. We might have been searching for them for weeks."

"Well, we can't have escaped prisoners wandering about the countryside," replied Helda. "After all, they might go breaking the law. Now, Governor, I have a little favour to ask you."

"Yes, Miss Helda?"

"This pretty little slut here..." she waved her whip idly towards Lia. "She is a problem to me. So pretty, don't you think?"

The man walked round the desk to stand beside Helda. He ran his eyes over Lia's bare flesh, a slight sheen of perspiration on the top of his head, making it shine. Lia wondered if it was the sight of her that made him sweat so, or his nervousness in Helda's presence.

"Very nice," he said hoarsely.

"Yes she is, isn't she?" Helda reached out with her riding crop, teasing Lia's nipples and smiling as they became erect. "And so sensitive," she murmured. "But unfortunately she has been the bane of my life of late. Would you believe the little bitch escaped from me, and has been on the run for more than two months? And all the time as naked as you see her now. When I found her this evening she'd just had five men at the same time. Totally shameless!"

The Governor nodded, the beads of moisture on his head growing larger.

"What I need, you see, is to take her out of circulation for a time. There are others searching for her, and I need to take the heat off for a while. I have plans for this young lady, but I'm not ready to implement them as yet. That's where you come in."

"Me, Miss Helda?"

"Certainly. What better place to lose someone than incarcerated in here? After all, some of the lowlife inmates of this prison are never seen again, for one reason or another."

The governor blushed. "I can assure you..." he began, but Helda raised her hand.

"Never mind that," she said. "The fact is, I want you to take charge of her for the time being."

"But..."

"No buts. She is to be kept here and treated like any other prisoner."

"But she's... she's female."

Helda smiled condescendingly. "You noticed?" The smile vanished. "Now, I want a strict regime. She must be kept busy and kept fit. She is to be caned regularly. Do you understand?"

"Yes, Miss Helda." At the mention of the caning the Governor's eyes widened.

Lia was listening to the conversation with growing dread. So that was Helda's plan. She was to be locked up. She had been expecting to be returned to the Black Cat. The thought of being in prison was a fearful one.

Helda rose to her feet. She took Lia's breast in her gloved hand, the feel of the leather on her soft flesh making the girl gasp. Helda kissed her on the lips, her tongue darting into Lia's mouth while her hand continued to knead her breast. Lia responded to the kiss, her legs going weak at the sensation of Helda's tongue wrapping around her own, but Helda broke away, laughing.

"All in good time, pretty one," she said. She turned to the Governor. "See how responsive she is? I'm sure she'll give you lots of fun."

The Governor was watching, his mouth slightly open, his crotch bulging.

Helda beckoned to her companions and made for the door. As she reached it she turned back. "One other thing," she said.

"Yes?"

"Keep her naked. I think she likes it, and I know I do." With that she was gone.

Lia turned to look at the Governor. He was already unbuttoning his pants.

Chapter 26

It was three months before Lia left the prison. Three months of hard work, punishments and sex. She was locked in a cell at night and made to mix with the other inmates during the day. To chronicle her adventures totally would take another book, and perhaps one day that will be written, but suffice to say her naked body was beaten and fucked by staff and prisoners alike, that she spent hour after hour crushing stones, digging trenches and waiting on the staff. And all the time she took a perverse pleasure from her treatment, occasionally reaching orgasm simply from a groping touch, or the bite of a cane across her arse.

But never a day went by when she didn't think about Thorkil, and wonder if he was still searching for her, or had given her up for lost and was even now sharing his bed, and his belt, with some other girl.

On the day they came for her it was totally unexpected. She had been working outside on a chain gang cutting wood when she was ordered to go straight to the Governor's office. She knocked on the door with trepidation. Normally such a summons meant a caning, followed by the Governor's cock pumping into her while she lay face down across his desk. So it was with a start that she found Helda sitting in his chair again, smiling sweetly at her.

Lia went to the desk, her hands immediately going to the back of her head, and stood silently, waiting to see what would happen. Helda rose and approached her, walking round her and inspecting every inch.

"Very nice," she said at last. "Very nice indeed. Prison life seems to have suited you."

Lia blushed. There was no doubt about it, the prison regime had done her some good. She had a lovely tan, not too dark, but covering her all over. Her body was even more lithe than before, the hard work and strict diet toning her muscles to perfection. Even her breasts were firmer, as the result of constant lifting of heavy weights. Her pubic hair had grown back, though she kept it carefully trimmed on the orders of the warders. All in all she was a picture of beauty, the stripes across her bottom simply enhancing the effect.

"Good," said Helda, and the Governor beamed, clearly pleased with her response. "Now, young lady, are you ready to leave?"

"Yes Mistress." Lia's reply was given with mixed feelings. Though the prison life had been hard and demanding, as with all things she had grown used to the routine. Returning to Helda meant the unknown. She was certain she was not going back to the Black Cat. Helda had intimated as much before leaving her at the prison. So it was with a beating heart that she followed the woman out through the great doors to where motorcycles were parked.

The journey was a long one, but Lia didn't mind. It felt good to be away from the dark and gloomy fortress in which she had spent the past quarter year and sitting there, manacled to Helda's machine, the wind blowing through her hair, she felt almost carefree.

It was almost evening when the bikes left the highway and headed off down a minor road that twisted and turned until it ended at a large building. It was a tall brick affair, with none of the brooding gloom of the prison. Lia guessed it was an old manor house, not unlike the Black Cat, but smaller. As they unshackled her from Helda's bike she looked about, taking in the beauty of the location. In front of the house was a lawn that led down to a lake. Beyond was a thick forest that seemed to stretch for miles into the distance. But she wasn't given much time to admire the view. Helda was hustling her into the house.

Inside she was surprised by the decor. Despite its rich exterior it was sparsely furnished, the floors and walls bare, so that the great entrance hall echoed to the sound of the Bikers' boots as they strode in. On one side a pair of double doors were open, and sneaking a glance inside Lia could see masses of wires and strange shaped pieces of equipment, none of which meant much to her. She had no time to take a closer look as she was taken through the doors on the other side, through an equally bare room, then down a narrow staircase to the basement, where she was led into a small stone cell. On the floor was a mattress, and chains hung from the low ceiling. They stood her against one wall, attaching her wrists to manacles, then without a word they left her, closing the door and plunging her into darkness.

She had no idea how long they left her standing there, her muscles cold and cramped, chained to the rough wall. In the darkness the passage of time was impossible to gauge, but at last she heard the sound of someone outside the door. A key grated in the lock then it swung open, the shaft of light from outside illuminating her body as she hung there.

"Hello again."

She recognised the voice at once. It was Delgado, standing with hands on hips, grinning at her. "So nice to have you back," he said. "Now come on, I've got to get you ready. There's some very important people here to meet you."

He undid her shackles and led her from the cell. They ascended the stairs and he took her into a large kitchen, with a huge old range on which pans were bubbling. A cook was stirring one of them, and she eyed Lia with distaste.

"This is her, I presume," she said.

"This is her," replied Delgado. "A plate of your best game pie please, Mrs Barnes."

The woman gave a snort, and bent down to open the oven door. She scooped a generous portion of pie onto a plate, then set it round with vegetables and potatoes. She placed it on a table on one side of the room.

Delgado pulled back a chair and indicated to Lia to sit. She ate hungrily, savouring the richness of the food after the spartan fare she had become used to in the prison. Delgado poured her a glass of red wine and she quaffed it down, enjoying the warm feeling it gave her.

Once she had finished she was allowed to use the bathroom to wash and tidy her hair. Then her hands were cuffed and she was led back through the house.

Most of the building was deserted, and rather gloomy. Clearly it hadn't been lived in for some time. At the end of one of the corridors a light was creeping out from under a door, and beyond it Lia could hear voices. She hesitated, suddenly shy of exposing herself to whomever was within, but Delgado simply swung the door open and pushed her inside.

The room was brightly lit and smoky. Helda sat in a large chair by the far wall. Beside her was an enormous man wearing the leathers of a Biker. Despite him sitting Lia could see he was well over six feet tall, with a huge beer gut that hung over his pants. His face was almost completely hidden by a vast bushy beard, and his eyes glittered below thick eyebrows. Beside him sat a number of other Bikers Lia did not recognise, as well as those who had accompanied her and Helda from the prison.

"Ah, here she is," said Helda, a smile spreading across her mouth. "Lovely, don't you think, Horst?"

The fat man licked his lips. "Very nice," he said, and the other members of his entourage mumbled their agreement too.

"But how rude of me," went on Helda. "I haven't introduced you. Lia, this is Horst. He's a film producer."

Lia said nothing as Horst studied her body, his eyes roving over her firm breasts and neat pubic bush.

"Yes, my dear," went on Helda. "We've been making lots of plans for you over the last few months. You see, I have an idea that's going to make you very well known, and me very rich."

Helda nodded to the young man next to her, and he threw a pile of magazines and books at Lia's feet.

"Go ahead," said Helda. "Read them."

Lia stooped and picked up the first magazine. She had seen it before. The warden had shown it to her just before her escape from the Black Cat. It depicted her in the diner, on the table, masturbating with the bottle. The copy was lucid and lurid. She put it aside and picked up another. This again pictured her in the diner, spread-eagled against the mirror, with the officer's fingers firmly inserted in her sex. The look of passion on her face told it all. She picked up a third. This was a popular tabloid newspaper, and the cover picture displayed her bent over a chair at the Black Cat, as a man beside her wielded a cane. The headline read *Where is Kinky Lia?* and went on to describe how she had disappeared after her escape from the Black Cat. Inside there were more photos, and detailed descriptions of what went on at the Black Cat.

There were more. A surprising number. It seemed to Lia that her naked body had appeared on the front of most of the newspapers in the land.

"You see," said Helda, "we've made you quite a celebrity. Almost anybody who reads that sleaze knows your name, and that you're missing. There have been some quite interesting theories as to where you've gone. None of them correct, of course."

Lia was barely listening. She was staring at the depictions of her naked body that had been circulated everywhere. She wondered what her former colleagues in the factory and the hostel must think, when they saw her baring her breasts and sex so publicly. And yet at the same time there was something erotic about the idea of all those people ogling her, and suddenly she had an image in her brain of a young man holding one of the magazines in his hand whilst wanking. She imagined him coming, his semen splashing across her photo, and an odd thrill ran through her body. She shivered slightly, a reaction not missed by Helda.

"See?" she said to her friends. "She's turned on. I said she would be."

Lia said nothing, trying to blot the image from her mind as Helda spoke again.

"Well, now we've got the public interested we're going to cash in. Horst here is going to make a film. A film about your adventures. And you're going to be the star."

Lia stared at her in amazement. So this was what she had been preparing! Her stomach churned at the prospect. She had little doubt as to the type of film they would make.

"We start shooting tomorrow," went on Helda. "Of course we've had to change the story slightly. Your little mishap being washed away by the river would be too hard and dangerous to film, so we've decided you're going to be caught trespassing instead." She turned to Delgado. "Have you organised the men who catch her?"

Delgado grinned. "No problem. There's a gang of lumberjacks working in the forest about half a mile away. I had no difficulty persuading three of them to take part. And they've got their own horses."

"Excellent," said Helda. "Well, my dear, it's time you were back in your cell and chained for the night. You've got a big day tomorrow."

Chapter 27

The scene depicts a pile of clothes lying on the ground. They are a woman's clothes. A singlet and shorts, bra and pants. As the camera pulls back we see a campfire, beside which lie a few tins. The camera pans to the right, and a picturesque lake fills the screen. In the middle someone is swimming, though at present their shape is vague.

The credits appear as the camera slowly zooms in on the figure. By the time the director's name has come and gone we can see the swimmer is a beautiful young girl, and as we watch she rolls onto her back, kicking out so that her body rises to the surface.

She is completely naked. Even at this distance we can discern firm breasts and dark pubes. She is swimming towards the shore.

The camera moves back to the campfire, and the pile of clothes, with the swimmer still just visible in the background, though out of focus. As we watch an arm appears from the left of the screen, thick and hairy with a tattoo just above the wrist. We do not see his face or body, simply the arm as it reaches for the clothes.

The hand picks up the panties, turning them over and rubbing the material between the fingers. Then with a single gesture it tosses them onto the fire, where they flare up with a bright flame. The bra, singlet and shorts follow in quick succession, each burning rapidly. The arm is withdrawn and the focus changes to the girl.

As the camera zooms in on her she rises to her feet, and for the first time we see her breasts in all their glory, the nipples hard and puckered from the chill of the water. She walks toward us, filling the whole frame, and we wait with anticipation for the lower part of her body to be revealed.

We are not disappointed. Her waist is slim, her belly flat, her mons covered by short dark hair. We can discern the pink of her sex. She is almost completely clear of the water now, walking up the beach naked and innocent, unaware of what lies in wait for her.

She reaches the fire and a puzzled expression crosses her face. She looks about, searching for her clothes. Her eyes fall on the fire and she gives a cry of dismay. She tries to rescue her garments with a stick, but they are beyond saving.

The camera pulls back, and behind her we see two men emerge from the bushes. They are tall and strong, naked to the waist, their chests bristling with dark curly hair. Like the arm seen earlier they are tattooed, their faces rough and unshaven.

Another figure steps into the frame in front of the girl. "Oh!" she cries, wrapping one arm across her breasts as her other hand drops to cover her crotch. The man is similarly dressed to his companions. The three could be brothers.

"What do you think you're doing, swimming in our lake?" the man asks sharply.

"Your lake?"

"That's what I said."

"I'm sorry. I didn't know it belonged to anyone."

"All the land round here is ours. Right up to the edge of the forest. You're trespassing."

"I'm sorry," she repeats.

"Sorry's no good. Round here trespassing's a pretty serious offence. We horsewhip trespassers in these parts."

"Horsewhip?"

"Yeah. Now come here."

He takes a step toward her, and she edges slowly backward. She gets no more than two steps when she is grabbed from behind by the other two. They pin her arms behind her back, revealing her breasts and sex once more. She tries to struggle but to no avail. One of the men produces a coil of rope from his belt and they force her back against a tree, where her arms are tied behind the trunk. The three men stand back to admire their captive.

"OK, sister," says the first man, "what the fuck are you doing here?"

"I was just camping," she replies in a small voice. "I didn't know it was private property."

"Of course it's private. All the land round here is."

"Well, I'll leave then."

"Damned right you will. But not before you've been horsewhipped."

"But you can't!"

The man moves forward. The camera goes into close up on his hand as he runs it over her breast. She makes a small mewing sound as her nipple hardens. The camera stays close as his other hand slides down her tummy. She clamps her legs shut.

Smack!

He spanks her thigh. "Open your legs," he barks.

She complies and he slides his fingers into her slit. He moves his hand back and forth and she groans. The camera moves to her face. Her lips are slightly open and she is breathing fast. We return to a close up of her crotch. His fingers are wet and her hips are beginning to move, shoving forward against his hand. The man turns to his companions and grins slyly.

"Go and get the horses," he says. "We'll run her off the land."

He withdraws his fingers. The girl is panting, her face flushed. The camera lingers on her crotch, the wet lips glistening in the sunshine. He wanders across and kicks out the embers of the fire, stamping them down then emptying a can of water on them. The water condenses in a cloud of steam, making a hissing sound. Behind him the men are approaching with three horses in tow.

One of the men disappears behind the tree and the girl's wrists are freed.

116

She stares around, and for a second we think she is going to try to escape. Clearly the man thinks that too, and grabs her by the arm. Her hands are bound in front of her. She stands, her hands over her crotch, staring at the three men as they saddle up their horses. The camera again moves in, panning down her body, over the lovely breasts and down to her sex, and we discover that she is touching herself, her fingers teasing her love bud as she waits. The scene moves back to her face, and her arousal is obvious.

Then they are off, the horses at the trot, their captive forced to break into a run behind them. We follow her through the wood, tripping and stumbling as she struggles to keep up with the horses, her breasts dancing as she runs. On and on they go, pulling her along behind them. Occasionally she falls, but they do not trouble to check their horses, simply dragging her through the grass until she finds her feet again and runs on.

The scene changes to the edge of the wood. We are shown a fence, topped by barbed wire. There is a gate in the fence, above which a worn notice reads *No Trespassers*. We hear the sound of hoof-beats, and through the trees we see the three horsemen approaching, dragging the hapless girl behind them. They rein the horses to a stop beside the fence and jump down. The camera lingers on the girl, whose exhaustion is clearly not feigned, her breath coming in great gasps as she struggles to regain her composure.

One of the men takes the end of the rope to which she is tied and drags her across to the fence. It is about ten feet tall and is formed of strong metal links, squares of thick wire about an inch and a half across. She is secured to it, her arms and legs spread apart and tied to the links. We see her pressed against the mesh, her breasts flattened, the nipples so erect they poke through. One of the men pulls a horsewhip from his saddlebag and takes some practice swipes, the weapon swishing through the air. The girl cranes her neck round to watch, an anxious expression on her face. She looks the picture of helplessness, her pert buttocks thrust back, a perfect target for the whip.

Swish! Whack!

It strikes squarely on her creamy buttocks, leaving a thin white stripe that at once begins to turn red.

Swish! Whack!

Down comes the whip again. This is no simulation. Both whip and backside are real, and the crack of the leather on bare flesh rings through the trees.

Swish! Whack!

The anguish on the girl's face is obvious as her body is thrown against the fence by the blows. Then the camera drops and we are treated to a view of her open sex, and as another stripe is laid across her arse a sheen of wetness is visible on the lips.

Swish! Whack! Swish! Whack! Swish! Whack!

The beating goes on, the blows forming a regular tattoo as they crack down on the girl's behind. We watch her from all angles, no part of her body hidden from our view as her punishment is meted out.

The beating ceases and the man throws the whip aside. The girl is hanging limply from the fence, her chest heaving, her backside striped red. Yet when we see her face in close up the expression is not one of pain, but of passion, so that as the man slides his hand between her legs and feels her sex the cry from her lips is one of pure lust.

"Jeez, the bitch really wants it," the man says, staring at the juices covering his hand.

They waste no time in cutting her down from the fence. Once free she drops to her knees. One of the men loosens his pants and his cock springs out, thick and hard. The kneeling girl does not hesitate, wrapping her fingers round the shaft and pulling it into her open mouth, sucking noisily.

The man sits down on the grass and she buries her face in his groin, her head bobbing up and down. We are presented with the perfect view of her red and punished arse. Her legs are spread, her sex invitingly open. As we watch another massive cock probes at her hole. The camera closes in as the man's rigid weapon sinks into her and the muscles of her sex close about his shaft. Then he is fucking her hard, shaking her body with his efforts, making her breasts swing beneath her as she continues to fellate his companion.

The sex goes on and on, the three men taking her in every position imaginable, with none of it missed by the camera's probing eye. The girl shouts and screams as she enjoys innumerable orgasms, none of them faked. By the end she is covered with mud and spunk, her breasts shining with the glutinous fluid that mats her hair and trickles from her cunt.

At last they are sated and they lift the girl up, carrying her through the gate and depositing her on the ground outside. Then they return to their horses and remount, riding off into the wood with barely a backward glance.

The camera lingers on the girl. She is lying on her back, her legs spread. As we watch her fingers creep down to her crotch and she begins to masturbate. The shot pulls back from the writhing figure, panning upwards toward the treetops as once again she orgasms, her cries ringing through the trees.

The picture fades.

Chapter 28

The filming went on for four weeks, during which time Lia was made to relive all her adventures between leaving the city and her time at the Black Cat, with a few variations thought up by Helda thrown in. They recreated the scene in the diner, using a real diner with real truckers, who shouted their delight as she brought herself off in front of them. The scene in the truck cab, where she had been sold to two truckers and took them both on at once was also repeated. In fact all her sexual encounters and punishments were recreated in detail under the cold eye of the camera lens, up to and including her first night at the Black Cat, with the raffle, the public whipping and the subsequent gangbang.

For Lia it was a bittersweet experience, her body kept in a state of constant arousal by the succession of fuckings and beatings she received on the film set. By the end of the fourth week she was exhausted, and glad to see the final shot in the can.

There then followed a period of relative quiet for the girl. She spent her days doing the housework or assisting the cook, and the nights chained in her cell. During this time she saw nothing of Helda, who she felt sure was no longer at the mansion. Occasionally Bikers would stop by, but otherwise her only companion was Delgado, who supervised her but never touched her. Clearly he was under orders.

The days passed and Lia fell into a routine she found quite pleasant after the gruelling time she had experienced previously. She was no longer beaten, and for the first time in ages her backside was free of blemishes. In the afternoons she would be allowed to lie in the garden, always tethered by an ankle to a post, and by the end of another four weeks she looked fitter and more tanned than ever. During all this time she was not touched, and was forbidden to masturbate, not an easy prospect for one of Lia's desires, particularly since she still spent her days naked. During the filming she had once again lost her pubic hair and her bare cunt often ached to be touched or penetrated.

Then, almost six weeks after the departure of the film crew, Helda came back. It was quite unexpected. One minute Lia had been relaxing in the sun, the next a shadow fell across her face and she opened her eyes to find the woman Biker standing over her.

"So here you are," said Helda. "My, they've been pampering you, haven't they?"

"Yes, Mistress."

Thwack!

Helda's riding crop swiped hard across her thigh, making her jump with surprise and pain.

"Don't you stand up in your Mistress's presence?" she snarled.

Lia leapt to her feet, cursing herself for allowing her guard to drop so easily. She stood stiffly, hands behind her head.

"That's better," said Helda. "We can't have you forgetting your training. I'll have a few words with Delgado. Why, by the look of that backside you haven't been beaten for ages. Has he been fucking you?"

"No Mistress."

"And have you been frigging yourself?"

"No Mistress."

"Good. Give me your cunt."

Lia had not heard the command since her days at the Black Cat, but she remembered only too well what was required of her. She thrust her hips forward, bending her knees slightly in a lewd gesture of submission.

Helda reached out, running her hand between Lia's legs and sliding a finger into her. The reaction was electric; Lia's whole body stiffening, a moan escaping her lips. She had almost forgotten how delicious it was to be touched so intimately.

"Mmm," purred Helda, "nicely on the simmer. Well young lady, your little holiday is over. Tonight you begin earning money once again. I'll explain it all to you after dinner." She turned and strolled away.

All through her evening meal Lia's stomach was so full of butterflies she could hardly eat. What could Helda have meant? A return to the Black Cat? The thought of going back to that place sent a shiver down her spine, as feelings of fear and pleasure ran through her. She thought of how she had been used there as a plaything for anyone who could afford her. Of the humiliation and the beatings. But she thought too of the way she had felt so stimulated, of the numerous orgasms, often many times a night, and a warmth crept into her groin.

Delgado came for her and led her to the room where all those weeks before she had been introduced to the film crew. Helda was waiting for her, along with two other Bikers she recognised from previous visits.

"Do come in, my dear," said Helda. "How was your dinner?"

"Very good thank you, Mistress."

"I'm glad to hear it. We have to keep you strong for what's to come. Would you like to know what's in store for you?"

"Yes please, Mistress."

"You remember all that publicity we organised for you? All those magazine and newspaper articles?"

"Yes Mistress."

"Well they're still interested. Look at this."

She tossed another pile of newspapers at Lia's feet. With a sense of foreboding Lia stooped and picked up some of them.

Biker's Girl Found! screamed the headline on the top paper, alongside yet another photo of Lia naked. She scanned the story. It told of how 'Biker sources' had informed the paper that Lia was back in the keeping of the owner of the Black Cat, and that she was shortly to star in a film of her own escapades. The other papers had similar copy, with speculation about the film itself and what would be shown, some of it clearly informed speculation. Lia read through a few more, then placed them back on the floor, her face red.

"You see? You're even more of a celebrity now," said Helda. "There's a lot of people looking forward to seeing you. Look at this."

She passed Lia a roll of paper. Lia unfurled it. It was a poster and she stared, her mouth open. It was a picture of Lia hanging naked from chains, while a fierce Biker laid a whip across her arse. All around were smaller pictures depicting scenes from the film. In one she was rising from the lake, and in another she was standing on the highway, one hand thumbing a lift whilst the other was between her legs. Across the top in large red letters were the words *Biker's Girl*, and below in smaller type *A new dimension in erotica*. Lia's colour deepened as she took it in. She rolled it up and passed it back to the smiling Helda.

"I hope you're good at public appearances," she said. "The film opens tomorrow, and you're the guest of honour. A personal appearance, no less. You'll enjoy that, won't you?"

Lia said nothing.

"Meanwhile," she went on, "we'd better put a few fresh stripes across that pretty little behind of yours. We don't want to disappoint your public. After all, they'll be expecting it. Now bend over that chair." She pulled her riding crop from her belt.

Chapter 29

Lia peered anxiously from the tinted window of the car as it swept through the streets of the city, a pair of Bikers in front and behind as escorts. This was the first time she had returned to the city since her escape from the watchman all that time ago, and it was strange to see the old sights again. Nothing much seemed to have changed. The streets were still strewn with litter, the shopfronts fitted with heavy metal shutters, gangs of youths gathered on every corner.

The car turned down a road that was very familiar to her. At the end was the shabby frontage of the hostel in which she had lived before making her escape and falling into the hands of the Bikers. She gazed out at it. She felt no nostalgia. Her life at the hostel had not been a happy one. Still, she wondered what the inhabitants would make of her now. When she had lived there she had been a shy and demure girl who kept herself to herself. What would they think of the naked beauty who sat in the car, her wrists and elbows pinned behind her, her breasts thrust forward as if inviting caresses? Yet she was still Lia, and the shyness had not gone. It was simply that she had discovered a desire within herself that she did not understand, but which drove her to accept, to relish even, the cruel treatment the Bikers dished out to her.

They swept by the hostel and made another turn. Lia recognised the area as one protected by the Bikers. It was an area she would not have entered in her days at the hostel. Despite the fact that the crime in Biker controlled districts was much less than in others, no young girl would ever have ventured there without an escort. Stories abounded of females being picked up by passing Bikers. At best they could expect to be released after a night of depravity. At worst they could be carried off and not seen again. And now here she was, right in the middle of the area, staring out at the men and women in leathers who patrolled the streets.

They rounded another bend and a huge building loomed ahead. It might once have been a sports stadium. Certainly it seemed far too large to be a cinema, though that was the legend in six foot high letters across the wall. But it wasn't that sign that caught Lia's eye. Above the entrance was a huge figure, a photograph, a vast cut-out figure that dominated the front of the building.

It was Lia.

She was sitting on the saddle of a motorcycle, her feet stretched forward, the toes pointed. Her hands were stretched behind her and cuffed to the back of the seat. She was totally naked.

Lia stared at the image in fascination. She had never seen anything like it. It was extraordinarily erotic. She recalled the day it had been taken. The photographer was so turned on he fucked her across the padded seat of the bike. She had never dreamed the shots would be displayed so publicly though. She glanced across at Helda, who sat beside her in the car.

"Do you like it?" she asked. "It's certainly caused a stir. The cinema will take three thousand people and we expect to sell every ticket tonight. Look, they're queuing already."

Sure enough, outside the cinema were hundreds of people queuing patiently in a line that ran alongside the building and round the corner out of sight. A set of crash barriers had been erected, along which patrolled a number of Bikers. The people gazed idly at the car as it passed. Lia wondered what their reaction would be if they could have seen who was inside.

They passed the cinema and sped on through the city streets, finally pulling up outside a reinforced gate. As Lia watched it swung slowly open, and the car purred through. They came to a halt outside a townhouse, surrounded by the high fence, with small towers overlooking front and rear. A man opened Lia's door and she stepped out. He took her by the arm and led her inside. Helda did not follow.

It was two hours later before she saw Helda again. In that time she was bathed, her hair was brushed and her face made up. Her hands were shackled as before and she was taken out into the courtyard.

There, parked in the drive, was the most magnificent motorcycle she had ever seen. It was covered in gleaming chrome, the paintwork airbrushed with scenes of Bikers riding along open roads in golden sunlight. The tyres were wide and fat, the exhaust pipes spotless and shining, sweeping up the machine on either side. It was almost a work of art.

Footsteps sounded from the house, and Lia turned to see Helda walking towards her. She wore the tiniest of miniskirts, made of fine black leather. She wore a short leather jacket, tailored perfectly to her shoulders and only reaching to just below her breasts, so that her midriff was bare. The jacket was joined at the front by a shiny chain which left it open about an inch, revealing bare flesh beneath. On her head was a cap, again of leather, almost military in appearance, and her eyes were shrouded by mirrored sunglasses. Lia had never seen her look so sexy.

She strode to Lia, the ever present whip dangling from her belt. "All ready for your big night?" she asked, then took hold of Lia's chin, looking into her eyes. "Now listen carefully," she said. "I want no funny business tonight. You're to do exactly as you're told. Do you understand?"

"Yes Mistress."

"And don't even think of trying to get away. My people are everywhere. All right?"

"Yes Mistress."

"Good. Now get on the bike."

Lia straddled the magnificent machine, the leather feeling smooth and soft against her backside. There was a click as her cuffs were fastened behind her to the seat. Helda too climbed aboard, apparently careless of the fact that her skirt rode right up in the process, baring the creamy white of the top of her thighs and revealing the tight leather thong that covered her sex.

The ride took them through the busiest part of the city. People turned their heads and pointed as they passed. They did not ride fast, so that passers-by were treated to a long look at the sexy woman Biker, carrying her naked captive along. Behind them rode two more Bikers, there to prevent trouble, their presence unnecessary. The people kept well clear of the machine, awed by the presence of Helda.

The bike swung round a bend and the cinema came into view. The image of Lia was brightly lit now, and as they came closer she could see the queue had grown, and now snaked round and back to the front of the building. Helda revved the engine and all eyes turned their way. Lia could see fingers pointing, and across the street cars were drawing up as their occupants craned their necks to get a view of her. Helda drew the machine to a halt and cut the ignition, and immediately Lia was able to hear the hubbub of the crowd as it surged toward the barriers.

Helda climbed from the machine, pausing to adjust her skirt before turning to Lia. "See that poster?" she said unnecessarily. "Pose like that."

Lia glanced nervously about. It had been one thing posing lewdly for a photographer, but this was quite another thing. She turned her eyes pleadingly on Helda, hoping to see a spark of mercy, but there was none.

"Pose," the woman said again.

Her face glowing, Lia slid her backside down the saddle, opening her legs a little wider. A wolf whistle sounded from the crowd, then another. Lia knew that every eye was upon her, and that what she was doing was totally brazen. There was a bright flash. Then another, and Lia blinked as a crowd of photographers pushed forward. Helda had invited the press.

"Look over here love!"

"Pout your lips. That's it."

"Raise your backside a bit higher!"

"Over this way. Push your tits forward a bit more. Great!"

"Lick your lips. Look as though you really want it."

Lia responded almost automatically to their demands, displaying her body to them as best she could, spreading her legs to ensure they could see the wetness within her. The cameras were exciting her, as they always did.

"Jeez, someone's been whipping her arse! Untie her, Helda, so we can have a good look!"

Lia's face reddened as she heard the request, aware of the sight that the stripes across her backside must make, and of the way in which they emphasised her submissiveness.

Helda undid the lock that secured her to the seat. "Kneel up on it," she ordered.

It wasn't easy with her arms pinned, but Lia managed to manoeuvre herself until she was kneeling on the machine, flash bulbs popping all around her.

"Press your tits down on the seat and raise your backside," ordered Helda.

Lia obeyed with an eagerness that was obvious, raising her bottom high, displaying the red stripes to photographers and crowd alike, a thrill pulsing through her sex as she realised what a sight she must make.

The photo session went on for a good ten minutes. Somehow the thought of the crowd gathered in the road, and the cinema queue filing past her just a few feet away made her position overwhelmingly arousing. The men and women's stares as they slowly made their way into the building were like physical caresses to the passionate young girl. When they made her straddle the front wheel of the bike she was able to rub her sex against the roughness of the tyre, small cries escaping her lips as her hips pumped back and forth. Helda spotted what she was doing and dragged her off, the watchers laughing, pointing at the streak of wetness left behind on the rubber.

At last the photographers were satisfied and Lia was ordered to stand beside the motorcycle. There then followed a news conference, still out in the street. The reporters shouting their questions to Helda, while Lia stood by her side.

"Why is she naked?"

"She prefers it that way. She has no clothes."

"None at all?"

"She has no need of them. She exists only to give pleasure with her body."

Lia pondered that answer. It was true, and in a way she felt proud of it. Who else could thrill so many people at the same time? If her function was to give pleasure, then it was a function she carried out very well. She looked at the faces of the reporters and saw that they hungered for her. She wondered how many people, men and women alike, would masturbate over her photos in the following day's newspapers.

"Was she forced into any of the scenes in the film?"

"Every orgasm depicted is genuine. She is an extremely sensual young person."

"And the punishments?"

"The beatings too give her pleasure. There is physical evidence of arousal after she has been whipped."

"Why is she shaved?"

"To keep her sex visible. To remind you of her desire to be fucked."

"Can't she speak for herself?"

"She speaks in the film, don't you my dear?"

"Yes Mistress."

The questions went on and Helda continued to answer them, somehow never admitting Lia's status as a captive, or her desire to be with the one she loved.

At last Helda called a halt. The doors of the cinema were closed now, and the Bikers were turning the unlucky ones away.

Taking Lia by the arm Helda led her inside. She took her along a dark corridor that led beneath the auditorium and into a small bare room. She released the cuffs, and Lia was allowed to stretch her cramped limbs. Helda stroked the girl's hair and checked her all over.

"Right," she said, "time to go to your premiere."

She led Lia up a narrow staircase. As they climbed higher the noise of the crowd reached her ears, faint at first, but growing louder with every step. Lia realised they were headed for the auditorium itself, and her pulse quickened.

The stairs ended in a door, and as Lia stepped through it the roar of the crowd hit her. She was actually stepping out onto a stage in front of the cinema screen, and before her were a sea of faces, all cheering and whistling. Helda took her to centre stage. She held up a hand and the deafening roar began to die down, until at last the auditorium was silent.

"As you can see," she began, "the star of tonight's show is with us!"

A cheer went up.

"Both she and I are as anxious to watch the film as you are, so I'll be brief. As you will no doubt have noticed, the best seats in the house are in the middle, there." She indicated a platform, set about halfway back down the auditorium. It was dead centre, the seats directly behind it removed since it would be impossible to see the screen from them. On each side of the platform was a divan, with one end raised, similar to those used by the New Age priestesses.

"I shall be using one of the couches," Helda went on, "and our star will be on the other. I expect there are plenty of you here who would like to join her."

A roar of approval went up from the crowd.

"Well, someone's going to be lucky!"

The crowd went silent, and Lia turned to stare at the Biker.

"Each one of you has a number on the seat in front of you," went on Helda to the hushed crowd. "We're going to draw a number..." her voice crescendoed, "and the winner gets to join our star during the film!"

Lia gasped. It was like her first night at the Black Cat all over again. She was being raffled. She glanced at the divan and felt an odd feeling in her stomach, which rapidly turned into a warm wetness in her sex. Somewhere out in the crowd was a man, or a woman, who would join her to watch the film. She watched as a Biker came onto the stage with a bag in his hand. He held it out to Helda, who dipped inside and pulled out a number.

"Two three seven nine!" she called theatrically.

For a moment there was silence. Then someone shouted out from the rear of the auditorium. Heads craned round as a figure rose from a seat in the balcony, hands held aloft. Lia squinted up. It was a man. Quite a young one as far as she could see, but before she could tell any more he had turned and was making his way down to the stage.

Helda led Lia forward, down a short flight of steps and up the centre of the auditorium. As she walked beside the seats hands reached out for her, groping and mauling. She did her best to ignore them, holding her head high as she made her way to the platform. She preceded Helda up to the raised area. The woman indicated the divan, and Lia nervously perched herself on the edge of it. She looked out at the faces below, waiting for her companion to join her. A figure appeared, making its way through the crowd, and she felt a sudden perverse thrill as she contemplated what was happening, her body tingling with anticipation after the weeks of deprivation Helda had imposed on her. Helda was smiling enigmatically at her, aware of her excitement.

The man had reached the platform and was climbing up. Lia saw him close up for the first time. He was older than she had thought, probably in his mid-forties, his hair slightly greying. He wore dark slacks and a casual jacket. He stood before her, eyeing her coolly.

Helda had risen to her feet as he approached, and she took him by the hand. "What's your name?" she asked.

"Jerry." His voice was deep and full of authority.

"Well Jerry, meet Lia. She's your date for the film."

Lia took his hand, her face glowing. It all seemed so oddly formal, shaking hands with the man as if they were meeting at a cocktail party, whereas she was naked in front of hundreds of people, and about to give her body to him.

The man sat beside her, and there was a break while the press moved in and more photographs were taken. He wrapped an arm around her for the shots, his grip firm. Her body tingled as he pressed against her, reaching up under her arm and toying idly with her nipple as the bulbs flashed.

The lights dimmed and the film began. The screen was huge, and Lia watched enthralled as her image emerged from the lake. Jerry sat, his arm round her, his fingers rubbing up and down her flesh. When the men began to whip her he took her hand and guided it to his crotch. She rubbed his pants, feeling the hardness underneath, and found her own arousal growing by the second. As the whipping continued his fingers slid down to her bottom, feeling for the marks of Helda's whip. He whispered in her ear, "Suck me."

The excited girl dropped to her knees, her fingers at his belt, pulling it undone. She slid down his fly and freed his cock from his pants. She fingered its thick shaft, marvelling at its rigidity. Then she lowered her head and began to suck on its swollen end, tasting his arousal. Out of the corner of her eye she could see Helda watching, and knew that many of the audience would be doing the same. From the screen came the cries of her first orgasm. There were many more to come.

"Kneel on the couch, with your tits over the end."

He spoke quite loudly, so that the people around them could hear. A mass of eyes turned in her direction as she released his glistening cock from her mouth and obeyed. She knelt on the leather surface of the divan, then leaned forward over the raised end, letting her breasts dangle invitingly. She spread her legs, presenting herself to him unambiguously. She glanced up at the screen, where she could be seen struggling through the diner with a tray of drinks as dozens of hands reached out for her body.

When he touched her sex she gave a cry of pleasure. It seemed forever since she had been touched there, and the desire within her was intense. She shoved her backside at him, revealing the moist interior, and grunted with pleasure as he accepted the invitation, sliding his fingers into her. She had neither expected nor intended to come so quickly, but the watching eyes and the sight of herself being touched up by the officer on the screen, combined with her recent deprivation, were too much for her. Suddenly her body was wracked by an orgasm, hoarse cries coming from her lips as her sex closed about his fingers, her hips pumping back and forth.

Seconds later he was inside her, his cock buried deep within her vagina. He began to fuck her. On the screen her alter ego was also being filled with a stout cock, this one belonging to the officer. In the film version he took her in the diner itself, in front of all the truckers, spread across a table on her back.

Lia's cries were almost drowning those on the soundtrack as Jerry fucked her enthusiastically. Eyes were turned in her direction, watching her breasts bounce as he rammed his groin against her. Lia knew she was putting on a shameful exhibition, but she didn't care. All she cared about was the cock inside her, and her own intense pleasure as it plundered her, the thrusts growing faster and deeper. She braced herself to accept his spunk.

He came with a shout, his sperm filling her, making her moan with pleasure, all decorum forgotten as her own orgasm overcame her. His hips went on pumping, shaking her body with their ferociousness as spurt after spurt of semen shot into her sex. At last she knew he was spent, his motions becoming slower and slower until he collapsed on top of her, pinning her to the couch.

The applause from the crowd rose in volume until a deafening roar filled the ears of the wanton, shameless girl as she lay, her eyes closed, her hips still slowly gyrating.

Chapter 30

For the next three weeks Lia spent every evening at the cinema, appearing at two performances a night. Each night she would have a different partner. She lost count of the number of times she achieved orgasm on that public couch. The auditorium was packed out for every showing, as news of the film and of Lia's performances spread.

Every two or three days Helda would have her beaten in order to keep the marks on her backside fresh. Sometimes she would do it herself, sometimes she would get another Biker to do it. Occasionally Lia was given the cane and ordered to choose someone from the queue to administer her punishment. She would be made to walk out of the theatre apparently unescorted, though the Bikers were always close at hand to prevent her escape. Once in the street she would make her way naked along the crash barriers as the crowd whistled and shouted, until she finally picked someone out and handed them the cane. He or she would then administer the beating in the middle of the street under Helda's supervision. Somehow Lia found these public thrashings intensely arousing, and from the moment the beating ended until she had a cock inside her she would be tense with desire.

It was in the fourth week that matters took a new turn.

The first performance had just ended. Lia's partner was a young labourer and he had taken full advantage of the situation, managing to fuck her four times during the performance, making her come again and again on the end of his rampant young cock. She was in the shower room, washing in preparation for the second performance when something flew over the top of the curtain into the cubicle, landing on the floor with a clatter.

Lia jumped at the sudden noise, swinging round to see what it was that had startled her. There, lying on the floor of the cubicle, was a stone wrapped in a piece of screwed up paper. For a second she stared at it, then she saw there was writing on the paper. Hurriedly she snatched it up before the water could wash the words away. Her heart racing, she unwrapped the stone and studied what was written. The ink had run slightly, but the message was clear. *Go to the ladies' toilet at 10 o'clock.*

She turned it over. There was no name, nor any way of telling who had written it. She peered out of the cubicle. Opposite was a window, open, but heavily barred to prevent escape. She crossed the room and looked out. She was on the first floor, and beneath was a courtyard where the dustbins were kept. The yard was deserted, but it was clear that anyone could have thrown the note from there, had they known where she was.

She read the note again. Ten o'clock! The second performance began at nine-thirty, so the film would be well underway by then. She wondered at the significance of the message. She was permitted to use the ladies toilet during the show, provided she was accompanied to the door by a Biker and spent no more than two minutes inside. Escape was impossible anyway, since like here the windows were heavily barred. Her mind raced. Of course it might be a hoax, or some sex-starved punter anxious to fuck her. But in the ladies' loo?

She glanced at the clock. Nine-fifteen. There was no time to ponder further. She had to be on her way. They would draw the winning number in ten minutes. Hurriedly she dried herself. Then pausing to flush the note down the toilet she stepped out to where the burly Biker guard was waiting. Ten minutes later she was in the arms of a middle-aged bank clerk, who was licking her breasts enthusiastically.

The man continued his attentions as the film began. Next to them Helda watched idly. She hardly ever attended the screenings now, but this was a night when Lia had been due for a beating so she was on hand to supervise. The neat red stripes crisscrossing Lia's backside testified to the fact that the punishment had been efficiently carried out. Tonight, though, her presence made Lia very nervous. Whoever had sent the message clearly didn't want Helda to know about it, and Lia's anxiety increased as the hands on the clock crept towards ten o'clock.

As the time grew close Lia was on her knees, the man's cock filling her mouth as she sucked it. He was moaning and she knew it would not be long before he would want to fuck her. She glanced sideways at the clock. It was one minute to ten. She raised her head, gently wanking him.

"Please, Master."

"What is it?"

"I need to visit the toilet, Master."

"Can't it wait?"

"No Master."

The man turned to Helda and raised an eyebrow. She gave a nod. Lia rose and slowly descended the steps to where her guard was waiting. It was dark in the auditorium and she picked her way carefully between the seats, oblivious to the hands that reached out to pinch and squeeze.

They reached the ladies' toilet and the guard checked his watch. "Two minutes," he said. Lia nodded.

She stepped into the toilet. The room was brightly lit, with a row of cubicles running along one wall and basins and mirrors opposite. At first she thought she was alone, but then she noticed one of the cubicle doors was closed. She stood, uncertain what to do. Should she knock on the door? What if it was a trap of some sort?

Her dilemma was solved by the sound of the lock on the cubicle door being undone. As she watched the door swung open and someone stepped out. Lia stared at the woman for a moment, then her jaw dropped in surprise.

It was the Countess.

She was completely naked, standing coolly as Lia's eyes travelled down her body. Her full breasts looked plump and inviting, her waist slim. The woman had shaved her pubis. Her mound was as smooth as Lia's, her slit revealed.

The sight of it gave Lia an odd feeling in her belly as she realised that her own pussy must be equally seductive.

She narrowed her eyes. There was something else different about the Countess. It was her hair. The style and colour were different from how she remembered. The woman must be wearing a wig. Lia opened her mouth to ask why, but the Countess put a finger to her lips.

"Hush," she said. "We haven't much time. Come here."

She beckoned Lia to stand beside her, and indicated the mirror on the wall. Then it struck Lia. The wig, was meant to make the Countess resemble her. So too was her nakedness, and her shaved crotch. Staring at her in this bright light the similarities were obvious. In the darkness of the auditorium it was quite possible they would be mistaken for one another, especially since, with her breasts, sex and bottom bare, it was unlikely they would be paying much attention to her face.

"Now listen, young lady," whispered the Countess. "If this escape is going to work you've got to do exactly what I say."

"Escape?"

"Certainly. You don't think I'm here like this for the good of my health, do you? Although I have to admit it is rather sexy." She giggled mischievously. "Feel how wet I am." She took Lia's hand in hers and guided it to her bare crotch. It was indeed very wet, and felt soft and warm and very tempting to Lia. She caressed the Countess's love bud gently.

"Mmm..." for a moment the woman seemed to forget her mission as Lia's fingers stroked her, but then she brushed the hand away. "We'll have plenty of time for that later," she whispered, regaining her composure. "Meanwhile we've got to get you out of here."

"But how?"

"The bars at the end window have been removed. As soon as I've gone climb through and wait in the courtyard."

"Where are you going?"

"Out there." The Countess indicated the door to the auditorium. "I'm going to play Biker's girl for the evening. And I can tell you the idea makes me horny as hell!"

"But what about Helda?" Lia asked anxiously. "She'll..."

"Helda won't touch me," said the Countess. "She wouldn't dare. I've got far too many friends in high places. Now pay attention. Once you're outside stay put and listen for the bikes. As soon as you hear them approaching run round the front."

Lia took the Countess's hand. "Are you sure you'll be all right?" she asked, sincerely concerned for the woman.

"Of course. What were you doing with your partner just before you came in here?"

"I - I was sucking his cock."

"A nice thick one, I hope?"

Lia blushed and said nothing.

"I'd better get going," said the Countess. "Now, you just look after yourself." She kissed Lia on the lips. "Good luck," she whispered, then she was on her way, her firm backside wriggling just as Lia's did as she set off out of the door.

Lia stood for a second staring after her, then she turned and headed for the cubicle. She pushed open the door and peered through. Sure enough the bars had gone from the window. She climbed onto the lavatory seat and looked out. The courtyard was deserted. She took a final glance back, then levered herself onto the sill, crouched there for a second, then dropped to the ground outside.

For a second she remained where she was, perfectly still and listening hard. There was nobody about. She straightened and made her way across the courtyard. She took a quick glance round the corner. The road seemed empty. She leant back against the wall, her ears straining for the sound of a motorcycle. All she could do now was wait.

In the auditorium the Countess had run the gauntlet of the audience and mounted the platform, where Lia's companion still sat, his erect cock jutting from his flies. The Countess held her head down as she approached, not looking towards Helda. As she reached him she dropped to her knees and took him into her mouth, letting the long tresses of the wig fall across her face, obscuring it from view. She began to suck, her head bobbing as the man gave a sigh of satisfaction. So far everything seemed to be going like clockwork.

"On the couch."

At first the Countess barely heard the command.

"I said on the couch."

She realised he was addressing her. Still keeping her head low, she rose to sit beside him.

"On your hands and knees, and get that arse of yours up in the air. I want to see everything."

The Countess felt a thrill of pleasure at the command. When they had made the plan she vowed that if she was going through with it she might as well enjoy it. She perched on the couch, deliberately facing away from Helda. Then she pressed her breasts down against the surface, raising her arse for the man. She gave a little gasp of pleasure as his fingers penetrated her.

He frigged her for a minute or two, sliding his fingers in and out, feeling the heat and wetness welling up inside her. The Countess was very aroused, her hips pumping back and forth in anticipation of the fucking she knew was to come.

"Raise your cunt higher."

It was when he made this demand that Helda glanced across at them. The Countess made quite a sight, her lovely rounded backside raised for the attention of her lover, her gaping sex stretched wide to receive his swollen cock. Helda turned back to the film. Then she blinked and stared at the Countess's behind once more. Her eyes widened.

"Wait a minute!" she growled. "You!"

The man turned his head. He was crouched behind the Countess and about to penetrate her.

"Get out of the way!" Helda ordered.

The Countess remained where she was, her face buried in the leather of the couch as she felt the man move slightly to one side. She heard Helda rise to her feet, and the click of her heels as she crossed the platform. For a second there was silence, then she felt Helda's gloved hand on her bottom.

"Where are the stripes?" Helda shouted. "The bitch was whipped less than two hours ago. Where are the stripes?"

The Countess said nothing, her face hidden. She could feel the man's cock pressing against her backside again as he dithered, staring at Helda.

Helda grabbed the Countess's hair, trying to yank her face round. All she got was a wig. The Countess turned to face her. For a moment nothing was said as the two women stared at one another.

"You!" snarled Helda, incredulous.

The Countess giggled. "Expecting someone else, dearie?"

Helda opened her mouth to reply. Then closed it again. She swung round. "The toilets!" she bellowed. "That's where she went!"

She set off at a run, shoving people aside in her haste. The Countess's companion stared after her, his mouth agape. The Countess reached for his cock. Why not? There was nothing else she could do.

Lia was unaware that the escape had been discovered. She stood with her back pressed against the wall, trying to pick up the sound of the Bikers. Then she heard a shout. Across the courtyard a face appeared at the window. It was Helda.

"You!" she shouted, pointing at Lia. "Come back here!"

Lia's heart sank. Discovered. The plan had failed. She was back in Helda's clutches. Desperation gripped her. Escape had seemed so close...

But she had to go on. After all, the Countess had worked so hard on the plan, and she was so close to freedom. She couldn't stop now. She felt a sudden surge of adrenaline fill her veins, and without stopping to think she made a dash for it, heading out towards the open streets, oblivious to her nakedness.

The road at the front of the theatre was almost deserted, just one or two passers-by staring in amazement at the young girl who suddenly appeared from behind the building. She stopped at the junction for a second, looking right and left. Then she set off up the road, praying she was going the right way. She ran hard, not daring to look back, but aware that she was being pursued. She hoped desperately they would not have time to go for their motorcycles. The road was hard and her bare feet hurt and made a slapping sound as she sprinted along.

Ahead the lights were getting brighter and she could see there were more people about. Still she ran on, oblivious to the shouts and whistles of the people as she sprinted by, her breasts bouncing deliciously as she went. Behind her she could hear shouts and she recognised the voice of Helda, who must be pursuing her in person. And she knew it was only a matter of time before she encountered another Biker, who would head her off.

Then she heard it. The far off roar of a motorcycle. At almost the same time she saw three powerful headlights appear in the distance. The machines were rocketing towards her, and she was afraid they would not see her. She ran on in the centre of the road, waving her arms frantically. She could hear the footsteps behind her and knew Helda was close.

Just as the bikes were nearly upon her there was a screech of brakes, and together the three of them wheelied round so they were facing the way they had come. Lia felt a gloved hand touch her arm but she made a final effort, leaping onto the back of the middle machine. At the same instant the Biker dropped the clutch and the machine roared away. Clinging tight to the rider Lia glanced back. Helda was standing in the middle of the road, shaking her fists at the departing machines.

Lia didn't need to see the Biker's face. She could tell by the flowing blond locks that her rescuer was Thorkil. She hugged him, burying her face in his jacket as they sped through the streets toward the city gate.

They rode a long distance from the city before they pulled off the road into the woods. They put a good mile between themselves and the road, then drew up in a small clearing. The moment Thorkil dismounted Lia threw herself into his arms and they kissed long and hard.

"Oh Thorkil," she said at last. "It's been so long."

He smiled down at her. "But worth waiting for."

"Yes." She snuggled close to him. "Don't let me go again, will you?"

"I won't."

His hand dropped to her breast, kneading the soft flesh, feeling the nipple harden under his touch. He pushed her backwards, so that she sat on the rear of the bike seat, her legs apart as he slid his fingers down over her mound. Lia shut her eyes, a moan escaping her lips as his mouth closed over hers again. Then she felt a hard cock brush her thighs and looked up in surprise. At once she recognised Thorkil's companions - Rico and Lara.

Rico was standing over her, his fly open, his rampant cock jutting out from his pants, while Lara gently wanked him. Lia felt Thorkil's grip tighten on her, forcing her back over the seat of the machine. For a second she struggled, then relaxed as Lara guided Rico's thick weapon into her vagina.

She gazed up into the eyes of her lover. He was watching her closely as Rico fucked her, trying to gauge her reaction. She knew she should be outraged, but she couldn't be. She simply smiled at him.

After all, she was a Biker's Girl.

The Biker's Girl Trilogy

Biker's Girl

Lia couldn't believe it. He wanted to spank her like some naughty schoolgirl! She hadn't been spanked since she was a child, and even then never naked. She stared at him.

"Over my knee," he repeated.

Lia struggled to think of something to say, something to prevent the humiliation he proposed to inflict upon her, but it seemed she had no choice. Slowly, reluctantly she bent over him as he sat, so that her feet and hands touched the floor on either side of the chair, her bare buttocks stretched taut over his lap...

Set in the near future, this is the story of a beautiful young runaway who glories in sex and exhibitionism, and is an out-and-out sexual masochist.

Due to an unfortunate incident Lia is naked when she encounters a group of Bikers, and naked she remains through many painful yet erotic adventures, in which she revels unashamedly.

But when the Biker of her dreams sweeps her off her feet she is surely to live happily ever after as his submissive sex slave... isn't she?

Biker's Girl 3 - Decent to Debauchery

Lia straightened, rubbing her bum, the tears trickling down her face. She'd had much worse beatings since she became a slave to the Bikers, but almost never one so humiliating; the stinging in her bottom eclipsed by her extreme embarrassment as she glanced around at the leering customers.

Submissive damsel in danger Lia's sexual adventures come to an erotic climax in **Biker's Girl 3 - Descent to Debauchery**!

And both these titles are also available as paperbacks at **AMAZON**.